TERROR CELL

TIM CURRAN

SEVERED PRESS
HOBART TASMANIA

TERROR CELL

TERROR CELL

1

One grim, rainy April evening, the sheriff of Florence County, Wisconsin received a phone call from his dispatcher telling him something very strange was going on. The sheriff, whose name was Deuard LaBay but was known as "Dew" and never anything else, asked for particulars and was told that a 911 call had just been routed to the office. The caller was a man and what he said was short and very much to the point: *"I've taken the mine and everyone in it. They belong to me and I'm going to eat them one by one."*

The call was traced to the offices of Superior Mining which had workings due west of Mineral City. Dew told his dispatcher to give a call-back to the mine, but she already had and for some odd reason could not get through.

"All right," Dew told her. "Call the State Patrol and let them know what's going on. Then pull Woody and Jerry in. Tell 'em we're going up there. I'll be on-site in ten minutes."

Thirty minutes after he met his deputies, Jerry Hauser and Woody Stromm, in the parking lot of the county building, they were en route above Mineral City. Up there you could smell the pines and feel the weight of the hills rolling down at you. It was wild country, densely wooded, cut by narrow ravines and deep-pocketed hollows. A dank, clotted ice-mist rolled through the headlights of the county SUV, turning tree stumps and deadfalls into looming, threatening shapes. The road was slushy with melting snow dissolving into pools of mud and Dew took it easy. He kept his eyes on the road where they belonged. A light rain was falling.

"What do you think is going on up there?" Jerry said to him.

1

"I don't know, Jer, and neither do you. So let's keep our imaginations in check."

Woody grunted. "Probably a prank. You watch."

They were both nervous, practically ready to have kittens, and Dew did not blame them. After all, how could you listen to that 911 call and not feel it crawling right up your spine?

But he played it cool on the ride up because he had to. It was all bad enough and weird enough without letting his men see any cracks in his armor. So he listened to the occasional chatter on the radio and remembered that he had almost been ready to go to bed when the call came in. He was hoping dearly that it was all a prank, a false alarm, something of the known rather than the unknown. Because if it wasn't, then it was really hard to even guess what they might be driving into.

The road twisted and turned a few more times and there, coming out of the thin ice-mist, was the mine. Dew couldn't see much of it. Just the offices and Mess Hall, the Dry Room where the miners changed out of their street clothes and into their working duds. There were probably thirty vehicles out in the lot under the sodium lights. A skeleton crew, no more. As he pulled in front of the main office, Dew could see the sprawling shacks and outbuildings that climbed the hills above them, the old shaft houses and headframes rising up into the gloom. They looked ghostly in the mist, skeletal. All those workings were abandoned now, reminders of the days when men tunneled down deep into the earth to work the lodes. These days, Superior was an open pit mine.

Woody grabbed the mic. "Dispatch? This is five. We're at the mine location. Leaving vehicle. Please standby."

There was nothing but static on the radio, rising and falling.

"Shit," Jerry said. "Figures."

"Try again," Dew told him.

Woody thumbed the mic. "Dispatch? Dispatch? This is five. Do you copy?"

Nothing. Just that awful static coming back at them. A hissing susurration like wind blown through hollow spaces and subterranean catacombs. It almost sounded like breathing if you listened too long.

Dew grabbed the mic but got the same. Radio was out for some reason. Some kind of interference, that's what it was. "Probably the ore in the hills," he said.

"Sure," Woody said.

He tried the cell modem on the touchscreen laptop mounted below the Motorola Astro-Spectra radio, but it was not even receiving a signal.

Jerry even tried his Nokia. "Whatever it is, it's got to my cell, too."

They stepped out into the damp night. The lot was wet with potholes of standing water and mud, heaps of slow-melting snow. The sodium lights backlighting the mist made weird shadows seem to glide around them. Dew tried his Motorola handpack radio and got that static again.

Sighing, he said, "All right. Let's go see what this is about."

2

First thing they discovered, of course, was that the offices were buttoned up tight. It was Friday night after all. Probably wouldn't be opened until Monday morning. A lot of the other buildings flanking the parking lot had lights in their windows, though.

They went into the Dry Room which was hooked up to three or four other gray, silent buildings. Soon as they stepped in there, Dew knew it was empty. The sound of their shoes on the plank flooring echoed out and came back at them with an almost hollow sort of sound. The Dry Room looked much like a high school locker room with its rows of lime green lockers and benches, girly calendars on the walls. Most of the lockers had names on them. Most were locked-up. The few that were open held coats, lunch pails, hats, street shoes. There was a doorway in the back of the room with a sign over it: SHOWERS.

"How many they got working up here at night?" Jerry asked, kicking at some mud on the floor.

"They run a seven-to-seven shift, I know that much," Dew said.

Woody tried his handpack but it was more of the same. "Try your cell again," he said.

Jerry shook his head. "Just did. Still nothing."

Dew stood there, thinking. He was listening to the silence around them which in the back of his mind was the silence of tombs. He did not like it. It was more than just the desertion he was seeing, it was something else. Something threatening and ominous that he couldn't quite put a finger on.

"C'mon," he said.

He led them out of there, not liking the way their footsteps echoed in the stillness. He tried a few doors and they were locked and the one that was open led into a broom closet. He found another corridor, gun-metal gray like the others, and his deputies followed him down there. They were bunching up so close behind him he thought if he stopped suddenly they'd bump right into him. It was like Moe, Larry, and Curly here.

Another door.

This one led down a tunnel and Dew followed it, figuring it had to come out somewhere and it did: the Mess Hall. All these building were spiderwebbed together by tunnels and walkways. He stepped into the Mess Hall which was pretty big, set with scathed formica-topped tables and benches. Coke and candy machines were lined up against the wall.

It was empty as somehow he knew it must be.

Eight or nine lunch pails and picnic baskets were opened. Sandwiches and cups of coffee were set out. The coffee was still warm. Sandwiches had bites out of them. A bowl of soup was still steaming. A cribbage board was set out and a few hands of well-worn cards were lying next to it.

"What the hell is this?" Dew heard himself say, giving vent to the vague terrors in his mind.

Jerry said, "Like they all got up in the middle of their break and never came back."

"Gotta be a reason," Woody said. "Maybe something happened. Maybe something down in the mines."

Jerry just looked at him.

"Could be," Woody said.

But Jerry wasn't having it. He was spooked and he wasn't afraid to admit it. "I don't like any of this, Dew," he said. "I get the feeling this whole place is empty."

"That's crazy. Big place like this."

Jerry just shook his head. "This whole goddamn place…it's like the Mary Celeste or something."

"The what?" Dew said to him.

"It's a ghost ship," Woody said, shaking his head.

Dew rolled his eyes. "Enough of that," he said.

"They found the Mary Celeste adrift in the Atlantic," Jerry said, dropping his voice a few octaves without even being aware of it. "There was supper set out in the galley. It looked like the entire crew just got up and left in the middle of the meal. But none of them came back. The ship was deserted. It drifted dead and empty for months."

"Ah, that's bullshit," Woody said. "They de-bunked that one years ago."

"Not in the book I read."

"Didn't know you *could* read."

"All right you two. Enough ghost stories. This is real," Dew told them. "I don't know what the hell is going on here but we have to figure it out or bring in someone who can."

He walked amongst the tables, looking at the food laid out, the card game, the pegged cribbage board. He saw a newspaper with a partially-completed crossword puzzle in it. There was a pencil sitting there. It was all unbelievably strange. As Jerry said, it was like these men had gotten up in the middle of their break and just never came back. He found a cell phone. He picked it up, knowing full well that if this was some kind of crime scene that he was contaminating evidence, but he couldn't help himself. On the screen somebody had been texting:

8:15:27 Shell: u gotta talk to her i'm serious
8:15:32 Rip: this weekend
8:15:35 Shell: i'm serious she won't listen to me
8:15:42 Rip: i'll do it
8:15:43 Shell: i'm sick of being the only parent in this relationship
8:15:47 Rip: i said i'd talk to her i will okay
8:15:51 Shell: u say a lot of things
8:16:03 Shell: are u there?
8:16:12 Shell: hello?
8:16:32 Rip: gotta go something going on
8:16:39 Shell: what?
8:16:47 Shell: u there?
8:17:11 Shell: u alive over there?
8:18:36 Shell: Rip???
8:21:03 Shell: forget it

So something had clearly happened at 8:16…but what? That was two-and-half hours ago which would put it roughly just before the original 911 call had come in. But if that was true, why was the coffee still warm? The soup still steaming as if it had been abandoned ten minutes ago? It made no sense. Dew set the phone back down. All this speculating was getting him nowhere. It was only deepening his paranoia which was nearly bottomless by that point.

"Anything on the phone?" Woody asked him.

"No, nothing," he lied. "Some texting around quarter after eight, that's all."

"Christ, we're gonna be at this all night. I just know it," Jerry said.

"You got a hot date?" Dew asked him.

He shrugged. "Well, you know, I was supposed to meet Marianna for breakfast. She's flying down to Florida to see her sister tomorrow night."

"I'm guessing you won't make it."

Jerry grumbled under his breath and Dew tried not to smile. It wasn't eggs in the morning he was thinking about with a girl who looked like that Marianna.

They searched around the Mess Hall and found nothing of interest. It was very much like what Jerry had said of that ghost ship, Dew realized. Nothing was touched, no signs of violence…yet everyone was gone. It made no rational sense. *Maybe it makes more sense than you're willing to admit,* he thought then. It was incomprehensible and as he thought that, a voice of pure cop-logic spoke in his head telling him that he was jumping to conclusions and he needed to watch it. Something had happened, yes, but that didn't mean it was something weird and not in the book. There were plenty of possibilities. All he had to do was think of them.

Problem was, he couldn't.

He was drawing a blank and he was not a man who liked blanks. Things always had reasons, particularly when you were talking crime. If this was indeed a crime scene, and the jury was still out on that, then there not only had to be a reason behind this but motivation. Shadowy, twisted, but still there if you could only let yourself see it.

"Place gives me the creeps," Jerry openly admitted. "I ain't too big of a man to say that."

Woody grunted. "Nobody'd ever accuse you of that."

"I wonder what happened here? All these people, just gone. It gives you ideas. Bad ideas." Jerry let that lay and when no one picked it up, he grabbed it with both hands. "I don't know why, but I got that same feeling I had that night we went up to Dwight Rose's place."

"Enough of that," Dew warned him.

The whole Dwight Rose thing was still a very sensitive subject that no one much liked talking about. Five years before, it was discovered that Florence County had itself a monster. The sort that came out at night and made teenage girls disappear in the moonlight. The first was Theresa Cestaro, age fourteen. She was out walking her dog, a Shih Tzu named Muggles. Muggles came home, but Theresa never did. Three months later, Brittany Richt, age thirteen, dropped out of sight while returning from a friend's house. The final missing girl was Toni Lynn Wannamaker, age fifteen. Less than two weeks after the disappearance of the Richt girl, Toni Lynn's boyfriend dropped her off at the curb. He said he watched her walking towards the house, going around the back way as she always did. It was the last anyone saw of her.

Oh, it was a mess, all right.

The sort of mess that was far beyond anything the Florence County Sheriff's Department was equipped to handle. State Patrol detectives were brought in along with forensic teams and pretty soon the FBI were involved. Weeks passed and then months with nary a break. People were angry. They were frustrated. They were afraid to go out after dark. Then, as such things have a way of happening, the case broke wide open. Missy Curlew, the owner of Bell's True Value Hardware in the town of Florence, reported an unpleasant smell coming from the upstairs apartment she rented to Dwight Rose. She was afraid to use her passkey and go in. As luck—or bad luck—would have it, Dew got the call and went in with Jerry and Woody. They all knew Dwight. Everyone did. He was a mailman, a Boy Scout troop leader, and a girl's softball coach. Woody had gone fishing with him. Dew had had him over for backyard barbecues. He was well-liked, well-respected. The sort of guy who would have given you the shirt off his back, as the saying went. But there was another Dwight Rose nobody knew about and that night they met him. In the living room, in black crayon, Dwight had written the particulars of the girls he had murdered on the wall: their names, ages, hair color, eye color, and where he had buried them.

He was found in the shower stall along with the razor he'd opened his wrists with. He'd been there many days and the stink, of course, was horrendous as were the flies. The image of that had stayed hideously fresh in Dew's mind all this time—the bloated, blackening corpse covered in flies. A spider had spun a web from Dwight's agonized death mask to the showerhead above. It looked like a veil. There were dozens of leeched flies in it.

The case wrapped up quickly after that. The remains of the girls were recovered. Forensic analysis showed that they had been strangled. Dwight had had postmortem sex with each repeatedly. Why he did it or what his personal demons were, no one ever learned. The only clue to his state of mind was scrawled in crayon on the bedroom wall: THEY MADE ME.

Even now, years later, it was a touchy subject because Dwight Rose had many friends in the county and people didn't like to think of the boys in his Scout troop or the girls on his softball team and how any of them might have been his next victim.

The entire sordid affair carried a special dark significance for Dew himself in that it made him doubt his competence as a cop—something he had never done before—and it had, in its own way, culminated in the death of his wife.

But we're not going there, he thought. *I've got enough right now.*

"Let's take a walk," he said.

He led his deputies back down the tunnel and through corridors until they reached the Dry Room again. Then out into the original corridor they'd been in. He followed it to its end, going beneath an arch that opened into a little vestibule with a wooden ramp climbing up to a doorway.

"What is that shit?" Jerry asked.

Dew was seeing it, too. All over the ramp, a trail of something wet and almost gelatinous-looking like the mother of all slugs had inched its way up to the door. Whatever it was, it looked sticky. It was drying fast and Dew got the feeling that there had been a lot more of it earlier.

"Smells funny, don't it?" Jerry said, his leather belt creaking as he bent over, sniffing.

He was right. It had a damp, mildewed sort of smell to it. Like wet laundry dumped in a cupboard and allowed to molder. It was strong, almost acrid. Dew realized then that he'd been smelling it ever since they arrived. Not bad like this, but there. A ghost of it. As if something rank had passed, leaving its scent.

"Nasty," he said.

Woody just looked at him. "I think it smells kind of...good," he said.

They both looked at him.

"It's rotten," Jerry said. "You call that good?"

But Woody shook his head. "It don't smell bad. Kind of nice. Kind of sweet like vanilla."

"You're nuts," Jerry told him.

It was strange, very strange, but Dew didn't comment on it. But neither did he dismiss it.

"Well, don't step in it, whatever it is," he told his deputies, feeling the need to say something. "Must have spilled some kind of oil there. I don't need you two slipping on it and tearing an ankle."

That's what he said to them because it made perfect sense. But in his mind he had been thinking other things. Thinking that this stuff was unnatural somehow and it might not be a good idea to get any of it on you. Especially stuff that smelled like that.

You can smell it...it stinks. How can Woody think it smells good?

He didn't know, but he didn't like it.

Keeping to the edges of the ramp, they went up and found a little office through the doorway. It must have been the office of a shift boss. It was fronted by glass windows that looked out over a huge parking garage set below with big Cat dump trucks and loaders lined up in rows. They were immense machines and Dew figured the tires on them were taller than he was. They all had little ladders for the operators to climb up into them. The garage was fairly well-lit, yet still managed to look gloomy as all such places did.

There was no one down there.

Just the machines, overhead lights shining on concrete wet with puddles and slush. Not a damn thing else.

In the office, there was a door on the other wall and Woody tried it. It was locked. Funny…but when he first gripped it, it started to turn just fine. Then it wouldn't budge. That was funny, all right, but he decided not to mention it.

"Gotta be someone around here," he said.

Jerry licked his lips. "What if there isn't?"

"Gotta be."

"Okay, what if we go through this whole goddamn place— and that will take most of the night—and we find no one. Then what?"

Woody offered him a pale smile. "That will mean nobody's here."

"Ha, ha."

"All right," Dew said. "You ladies save the speculating until we have something to speculate on."

While Woody stared out through the windows, amazed by the size of the Cats parked down there, Jerry stood with his hands in the pockets of his uniform pants as if he was afraid to touch anything. Dew took a quick look around. Nothing of interest. Papers on the desk, folders, a desktop computer. A coffee cup. A file cabinet in the corner. A coat thrown over the back of a chair. On the opposite wall, there was a blown-up aerial photograph of the Empire Pit where all the mining was done these days. Ledge after ledge after ledge climbing deeper into the earth.

When he turned from the photo, Jerry had the coffee cup in his hand. He was staring into it as if he was looking for clues.

"Is it regular or decaf?" Woody asked him.

"It's still warm," he said.

"Means whoever it belongs to must've just stepped out," Woody said, pragmatic as always.

"Or something," Jerry said.

"Don't start that Mary Celeste shit again."

Jerry shrugged. "I don't have to: you're thinking it."

"Shit," Woody said.

Dew was liking all of this less and less. He did not know for certain that all the people were gone yet he could not shake the feeling that they were. That the Superior Mining complex was one vast graveyard and they could search all night long and never, ever find anyone.

"It's weird and you know it's weird," Jerry said.

"All right. Enough already—"

"Hey!" Woody said, peering out the windows.

They both turned to him.

He was pointing at the window. "I saw something down there. Something moved."

"Something or someone?" Jerry asked.

Woody just shook his head as if he wasn't sure himself. "I saw...I saw movement. A shape or something moved behind one of those trucks down there. I saw it."

"Well, was it a man or a mouse?" Dew said, looking down there, peering very intently and not seeing a damn thing.

Woody swallowed. "It...I don't know. A shape. It moved."

He and Jerry looked at each other and Dew could almost feel the unease passing between them. Their eyes were glassy with fear.

"You two stay here," he said. "I'm going for a look."

"Dew...let's stay together," Jerry said.

"Just stay here. Both of you. That's a fucking order. You reading me?"

They nodded.

Their faces pinched and pale, they watched him walk out the door, listening to his boots clomping down the ramp.

3

It took a few minutes for Dew to find a door that led out to the garage. By the time he did, he was sweating. And it wasn't from exertion so much as from the inexplicable feeling that he was being followed, that someone was watching him. He could feel their eyes on him, watching, waiting, scrutinizing, but never revealing themselves. Two or three times on his mad flight down dead-end corridors he could have sworn he heard footsteps just behind him.

But when he turned...nothing.

He came to the door and stepped through it and he was out on a platform looking over the garage and all the massive equipment parked down there. He took a set of iron steps down and just looked around. He could see the glass fronting of the office above, the faces of Jerry and Woody watching him very intently. He waved to them. They waved back. They were scared like a couple kids that had just heard a good ghost story and he knew it.

Thing was, Dew was beginning to feel the same way.

That was the trouble with being a cop. Regardless of the circumstances, regardless of how bad something was or how it scared the shit out of you and made your balls shrivel, you had to investigate. It was your job. You had to trace it to its source and look it in the face. That's what wearing the badge entailed.

He walked out across the wet concrete floor. The garage was huge. It ran for nearly a city block, trucks and heavy equipment lined up. A row of sodium lights far overhead threw uneven illumination that was orange-tinted and unnatural. Dew moved slowly, hesitantly. Though he had no reason to be cautious, his back was up. He felt that sense of danger worming in his gut and no amount of rational thinking would dispel it.

But what was there to worry about?

Plenty, he thought. *I'm worried that all the workers here really have vanished. I'm worried that we're going to find out why. I'm worried deep in my guts that when we find out why, we're going to join them.*

He moved along the row of vehicles, smelling diesel fuel and hydraulic grease, something in his belly pulling up tight. He clicked on his flashlight because there were too damn many shadows. As he did so, he tried his handpack again. Nothing but static. It made no sense. At the very least he should have been able to talk to his deputies but even that was denied him. He slid it back on his belt.

Just keep going. Don't think about it.

He kept in mind that his deputies were watching him—watching him intently, no doubt—and he couldn't let them see him sweat. He was really the only thing holding the three of them together and he had to keep that in mind. Play it cool, play it easy. That was the way. He cut back behind a dump truck into the shadows, playing his light about.

What the hell?

There was something on the floor. A boot. That's all it was. A rubber knee-high boot. Probably the sort the miners wore down in the pit. Green gum rubber. Dew told himself that it probably just fell off the back of a truck...yet, he wasn't convinced. *It's only an old boot for chrissake.* Yes, that's all it was. A perfectly innocuous sort of thing, but for some reason it made a finger of fear wiggle down low in his stomach. He went over there and kicked it. It fell over. There was no blood on it, no shank of bone sticking out, no reason to make him uneasy...yet it did.

In his mind, which was definitely working overtime by that point, he imagined one of the miners coming out here, searching for someone, *anyone,* and something...some nameless horror...plucking him from his boots.

Crazy bullshit.

He knew better than to be thinking shit like that—

He paused. He was hearing music. It was ridiculous, but there it was: a muted, tinny strain of music and it sounded like a children's song. Something he might have known once but now escaped him. Feeling panicky and more than a little disoriented, he walked around the front of the truck. His mouth was suddenly so dry he could barely wet his lips. Up in the office, he could see Jerry and Woody staring out the window.

The music played on.

It must have been coming from one of the vehicles. There was no other possible source. He pulled his handpack radio from his belt. *"Jerry? Woody?"* he said in a subdued voice. Again, there was nothing but static. He turned towards the row of vehicles. He started walking along them until he came to a huge front-end loader whose bucket could have picked up a house. He could hear the song more clearly now. As inconceivable as it seemed, he was certain it was that Scottish children's ballad "Comin' thro' the Rye." The very idea of something like that playing from the cab of one of these monstrous vehicles in the empty, silent garage was either laughable or the most terrifying thing his mind could conceive of at that particular moment.

The loader.

It was coming from the goddamn loader.

Dew stood there in the shadow of one of its monstrous tires, wondering what he should do. As a cop, he knew exactly what he had to do...but something inside held him back. It made him unsure. *Enough.* He started up the ladder of the loader, the rungs cold against his bare hands. The ladder led up to a little platform outside the door itself. He climbed up there, his stomach crawling in his belly. When he reached the top, he could hear the music clearly:

> *"If a body meet a body,*
> *Comin' through the rye;*
> *If a body kiss a body,*
> *Need a body cry?"*

It was fucking insane.

The windows of the loader were tinted. Flashlight in hand, Dew went over to the door, gripped the latch, and pulled it open. The music stopped instantly. The cab was empty. The keys were in the ignition, but that was it. The dash display was dark. But for one moment, as he opened the door, there had been an odor—sweet, beyond sweet, like pink cotton candy at a county fair.

Then it was gone.

He stood there, leaning into the cab, unsure if he had heard the music at all. He looked back towards the office. He was at eye-level with it now. He could see Jerry and Woody chatting away. They didn't even seem to be looking in his direction.

As he started down the ladder, he clearly heard a door slam shut. *Shit.* He scrambled down the rest of the way and ran along the line of trucks. It could have been the door to any one of them. He searched back and forth, but saw nothing.

Yet, as he waited there, flashlight in hand, breathing fast, he knew he was not alone. Whoever was in the garage with him was just behind him or ducking behind one of the trucks or skulking in the shadows. The silence was unbroken. Now and again he heard some slush fall from one of the vehicles, but that was it.

His heart was drumming in his chest, his jaws clenched. He was suddenly aware of how alone he was, not out here in this immense garage but up in the hills at Superior Mining. Such a desolate, distant place. Out of radio contact. He could smell the dirty slush under his boots, the machinery smells of grease and oil and diesel fumes.

He started to get angry.

Angry because he was uneasy and afraid and he didn't like feeling that way. It was a gross insult to who and what he was. Almost instinctively, his hand reached down and snapped the catch on his Beretta 9mm. The weapon filled his hand and gave him confidence. Dew wasn't the sort of cop that drew his gun very often. He was old school and you didn't pull your piece unless you were planning on using it, something all the kid cops these days just didn't seem to understand.

But right then…feeling the unknown circling him…he was ready to use it.

ALL RIGHT!" he shouted, the sound of his echoing voice startling him. "I'VE HAD ENOUGH OF THIS SHIT! SHOW YOURSELF ALREADY! IF I GOTTA DO THIS THE HARD WAY, IT AIN'T GONNA BE GOOD! YOU HEAR ME? IF I GET MY HANDS ON YOU, YOU AIN'T GONNA LIKE IT!"

More silence. In the back of his mind, he was nearly sure he heard something like a muted laughter that reminded him of a child pulling a prank. But that had to be his imagination.

Then, back near the loader, one of the trucks started up.

4

"So how long you think old Dippity-Dew's gonna make us wait here while he inventories the fucking dump trucks down there?" Jerry asked, looking through the papers on the desk which were mostly concerned with payroll deductions.

Woody sat down on the edge of the desk, sighing. "You know Dew. He's not a half-ass guy. He got the call to come up here and found nobody; he's not going to stop until he sniffs out what's going on. Even when the state boys arrive—"

"*If* they arrive," Jerry put in.

"—*when* they arrive, he won't let go of this. He'll keep shaking this rug until he gets all the dirt out of it."

Jerry whistled. "Man, I like that comparison. If there's one cop that's a human Dirt Devil, it's gotta be old Dew."

"He's thorough, I mean. If something happened to you, wouldn't you want him on the case? He never gives up."

"I'm not doubting that he's a good cop," Jerry said. "What I don't like about him is that anytime we run into anything, he leaves us out of it. It's like we're Boy Scouts and he's the troop leader watching over us. We're cops, too. It's our job to mix it up just like it's his. We should be down there with him instead of watching it through this window."

Woody sighed again. Jerry was an okay guy sometimes, but this wasn't one of those times. When he got stressed, he started pissing and moaning, ragging and nitpicking like some old woman.

"Dew's the sort of guy who leads from the front," he explained to Jerry. "He won't put us into anything that he wouldn't take on himself first."

"Boy, you sure worship the guy."

"It's not about worship, Jer. It's respect."

"Respect, he says. Shit."

Woody let that go. "Dew has been a cop for over thirty years, man. He knows his shit. Why don't you ease off and learn from him?"

Jerry giggled. "I should because it's all about R-E-S-P-E-C-T, ain't it?"

Woody ignored that, too.

Jerry was thinking about his girl. About breakfast in bed with Marianna. Woody figured he'd be getting pissy, too, if it meant missing a roll in the hay with that girl. She was tall and dark, legs right up to her neck. Those dark eyes, that smooth olive Italian complexion. *And let's not forget those tits. Jesus, they were something.* How was it shitheads like Jerry ended up with hot girlfriends?

True to form, Jerry said, "You're pretty palsy-walsy with old Dew, ain't ya?"

"Sure, we're connected at the hip."

"I'll just bet you are. I wouldn't be surprised if you make undersheriff now that Frank is retiring."

"Ah, I doubt it."

Jerry snorted a hollow laugh. "Oh, I don't doubt it. You and Dew are pretty tight. Pretty damn tight. Not that there's anything wrong with it. If I had it in me, I'd be kissing his ass, too, but I'm no good at that."

No, you're not, Woody thought. *You're not very good at anything, come to think of it.*

"Me and Dew have no chemistry. None at all. Besides, I can't suck dick just to get a promotion."

Ah, there it was: jealousy. That's what was at the core of this. Woody knew this could become an argument very fast, but he wasn't going to allow that. He would sidetrack things and there was really only one way to do that effectively with Jerry.

"I like Dew. He's okay. I need a role model." Woody winked at him. "Then again, I don't have a supermodel girlfriend like Marianna."

"You quit worrying about my girlfriend."

"I'm razzing you."

"You're always saying shit about her."

Woody stared at him. "Stop it, Jerry, okay? Just stop it. I've never said anything disrespectful about your girl and you know it. I'm kidding. Don't be a dick."

"Shit."

Jerry was nervous. This place was getting under his skin and he was reacting the only way he knew how: by being a pain in the ass. Woody knew he had to ignore him because Jerry would keep running his mouth until he got the reaction he wanted which was to piss off his partner so he wouldn't be miserable alone. Grace under fire was not Jerry's strong suit.

"Just wait it out," he told him.

"Shit," Jerry said again.

But it quieted him anyway. That was something. There were some things in life you just couldn't put a price tag on.

For some reason, Woody couldn't take his eyes off the locked door across the room. When he'd first tried to open it, he could have sworn the knob turned and turned easily...right before it seized up. It was almost like someone had grabbed it from the other side.

Oh, don't start with that shit, he warned himself.

Still, he wanted to go over there and try it again. But if he did that, it would tip Jerry that he was worrying about it.

Jerry stood up. He walked the few feet to the window and looked out. "Where the hell is he?"

Woody looked out there. All the trucks were lined up, but no Dew in sight. It didn't mean anything. The garage bay down there was huge.

"Maybe we should go look for him," Jerry said. "Maybe something happened."

"It's only been ten minutes or so. Relax."

But Jerry wasn't relaxing and neither was he. Dew wouldn't like it if they didn't do what they were told...still, what if something had happened? Woody rejected that. Or tried to. *Something* had happened to the people here. And that mysterious something could happen to Dew as well. He shook his head. *It would take one hell of a spook to get the drop on that guy.* Now why had he thought that? *Spook?* Why that word? He sighed yet again and continued waiting.

Jerry couldn't sit still. "This place is getting to me." He pulled out his Motorola. "Dew? This is Jerry, you there?" he said, his voice strung so tight with tension it sounded like it might snap. "Dew? You copy? *Dew?*" There was just static and then a sudden loud squealing burst. He nearly dropped the handpack. "Shit…did you hear that?"

Woody swallowed, then swallowed again. He was having trouble wetting his throat. "Just that…that ore in the hills like Dew said. Your signal bounced right back at you."

"Ore, my ass." Jerry practically had his nose up to the glass now. "This is fucked up and I don't like it."

Woody was staring out there now, too. He couldn't seem to stop. He had the most awful sense that something was building in the air around them like lightning getting ready to strike. The hairs on the back of his neck were standing on end. For one awful moment, he thought he caught sight of a spidery shadow moving amongst the trucks down there, but it was so quick it must have been a trick of the eye. Still, he was filled with apprehension and something quite near horror at the very idea of it. A wind rose up outside somewhere with a dismal moaning that made his hands shake.

"That's it," Jerry said. "We're going down there."

"Okay."

Woody led the way, glad to be doing something. He went to the door and grabbed the handle. He tried to turn it, but it was locked. He jiggled it frantically.

"Let me see that," Jerry said, breathing fast now. He jiggled it and jiggled it, putting all his strength into it but it wouldn't budge. "What the fuck?"

"It was open before."

"Yeah, I know it was open before. That's how we got in here." He fought with the knob and then in a fit of aggravation, he started ramming it with his shoulder and when that didn't work, he kicked it. "Fuck is going on here?" he gasped, his face red, his eyes bulging from his head. "This door was open! *I know it was fucking goddamn well open!*"

"Settle down!" Woody told him.

Jerry walked in a loose circle, kicked a wastepaper can out of his way, swearing under his breath, and then launched a violent assault at the door, ramming it and kicking it again. He cracked the panel and hurt his shoulder, but that was about all he accomplished.

"You done now?" Woody said.

Jerry rubbed his shoulder. "Yeah."

"Worse comes to worse, we've got sidearms, we can easily blow that lock off...but we better try everything else first because Dew will have our asses if we discharge our weapons for something like this."

"Dew, Dew, Dew. Christ."

Woody sighed. "Meaning?"

"Meaning you're obsessed with the guy. You act like he's your fucking dad. It gets old."

"Back to that again."

"Maybe," Jerry said.

"Okay, let's talk about your girlfriend then."

Jerry glared at him. "You're crossing the line."

"And I'm crossing it because you're being an ass."

Jerry turned away from him, staring at the door. "Look at the knob," he said.

"Yeah? What of it?"

"*Look,*" Jerry said. "There's not even a lock on it. There's nothing. It can't lock."

Woody knew he was right. He had been thinking the same thing but hadn't wanted to admit it. He stepped lightly over there and jiggled it. Still locked. He grabbed it loosely and tried to turn it in case it was matter of just putting a little English on it. No good.

Suddenly, he pulled his hand away with a gasp. "It's...it's fucking warm. I mean *really* warm."

"You're nuts," Jerry said. He gripped it himself and pulled his hand away. "It's burning fucking hot!"

And how are you going to explain that one? Woody asked himself, knowing damn well there was no reasonable explanation for it. Jerry was looking at him, waiting for him to frame this latest development in some rational way that would chase the shadows out of his mind. It wasn't so much a matter of him wanting it but *needing* it.

"You smell that?" Jerry said.

He nodded. "Like...like candy or something."

"Yeah."

It was more than just that, though. It was the way the inside of your Halloween bag smelled the morning after trick-or-treating, a wonderful, mouth-watering aroma of candy corn and chocolate, peanut butter kisses and salt water taffy, orange Jack-o-lantern suckers and skull licorice. That commingled odor of autumn joy that every kid knew and every adult still carried deep in the pleasure centers of their brains.

"It's crazy," Jerry said. "Nothing can smell like that...not here."

Woody opened his mouth to agree...but closed it just as quick. A series of loud rappings were heard in the walls. *Boom, boom, boom, bam-bam-bam.* Jerry let out a shrill childlike cry and Woody felt something cold, very cold, encase his heart in frost. It came again and then again. It was as if somebody was out there, running around and banging on the wall.

Jerry nearly came unglued. "STOP IT!" he called out, pulling his Beretta 9mm and aiming it at the door with a badly shaking hand. "I GOT A GUN AND I'LL FUCKING USE IT! SWEAR TO GOD, I WILL USE IT!"

Woody was going to tell him to put the gun away, but he didn't. And he didn't because he had slid his own weapon out now. He did it automatically, without thinking. The noises had ceased out there. In his mind, he was silently counting off the seconds. *One...two...three...four...five...six...*then it came again: *boom, boom, bam-bam-bam!* Jerry nearly fell backwards over the desk. As it was, he went down on his ass. He was mumbling something in a low, sobbing voice, quite near to a breakdown.

The banging stopped.

Again, Woody was counting the seconds.

Something bumped against the outside of the door.

Jerry made a whimpering sound. Using the desk, he pulled himself to his feet. His eyes were wide, white, and very wet. His lips were twisted in a snarl, cords standing out in his throat.

The doorknob turned back and forth.

Then it was jiggled madly.

Jerry let out a cry and opened up. He put three rounds through the door and the noise of that was almost deafening in the confines of the office. And in the back of Woody's mind, a little voice said, *oh shit, oh Christ, what if that was Dew out there—*

But it wasn't Dew.

Whatever had been standing out there, let out a squealing cry like a cat whose tail had been stepped on. They heard it retreat down the ramp with a clumping noise.

"Jerry," Woody breathed. "It's gone...it's gone..."

And with it, the sweet candied odor. It left behind a decidedly sharp, foul odor like vinegar.

Jerry tried to nod but he was shaking so badly by that point that his head just sort of quivered on his neck. Woody told him to put his gun away and Jerry did. Woody walked over to the door and tried the knob. It was no longer hot. And it was no longer locked. It moved easily in his hand.

"C'mon," he said.

Jerry nodded again and went to his side and then, behind them, they heard another sound. It was the sound of the other door, the locked door. Woody whirled around. The knob turned and the door slowly started to open.

And as it did, both men smelled something like a hot soup of blood fill the office.

5

Dew stood there with his gun in his hand, listening to the roaring of the truck's engine, the stink of diesel fuel which was as revolting to him at that moment as the stench of burning human flesh would have been. It was revolting because it did not belong and he knew it. It was unnatural and maybe more than that even—sort of low and coarse and evil. The idea of which would have made him laugh yesterday or last week, but he wasn't laughing now.

He knew he had to go see who started that truck.

Just as he knew that when he got there, there would be nobody in the cab. Nobody at all. Because this was some kind of fucked-up game being played.

What the hell?

He happened to glance up at the office and there was Jerry and Woody in the window, waving. It was obvious from the angle that they weren't waving at him.

Then who?

Dew looked around but there was no one, of course. Only him and the rows of vehicles and that nagging, horrendous feeling that he was not alone, that another was near, one that liked to play terrible games.

Jerry and Woody were still waving.

They're either seeing something you can't, Dew thought, *or are being made to.*

But as he pulled out his Motorola radio, he realized there was another alternative—they weren't really there at all. But the idea of that was confusing and he didn't have the time to muddle his thoughts.

"Jerry! Woody! I need you down here right now!"

Static was followed by the same whining squeal Jerry had heard. Dew grimaced. It rose to a high, piercing note that was like a silver needle puncturing his eardrum.

He thought: *You better go back up there. Anything could have happened to them while you've been chasing ghosts down here.*

Yes, and he *was* going back to them. But there was something else he had to do first. His entrails tangled up like hot mating worms, he started towards the running truck. It was down by the loader. By the time he got there, his heart was tapping wildly in his chest and there was no spit in his mouth. The Beretta felt very heavy in his hand and he wondered if he would even have the strength to lift it if it came down to it.

Oh, you'll lift it, all right, a voice told him. *If there's anything to lift it at.*

It was easy enough to find the right truck because its lights were on—headlights, cab lights. It was another Cat, though not as big as the loader. Still, he had to use a ladder to get up to the cab. One look told him it was as empty as he knew it would be. He pulled open the door and looked around. The keys were in the ignition, of course. He reached over and shut the truck off.

The moment he did, there was a crackling of static coming from the radio. But all the vehicles had radios. It didn't mean anything at all.

It crackled again.

Dew leaned into the cab, his flesh feeling like it was ready to crawl off his bones. His instinct told him to get the hell out…but his morbid curiosity wanted to know how this was going to play out.

"This is Three," a voice said over the radio. *"Pick up, Twelve."*

Sure, Twelve was stenciled on the door in big black letters. Whatever sort of vehicle Three was, it was calling him.

Another crackle of static. *"Pick up, Twelve."* The voice was a man's, deep and rasping but perfectly human for all that. *"You better pick up, Twelve. Your time's running out."*

Dew snatched the mic up. "Who the hell is this?" he asked.

More crackling. *"That's the big question, the one that can't be answered. Point being, my friend, you are in a real pickle here and if you want to survive this, then you better start doing some thinking. There's something here, Dew. Something that*

26

might be alive and might be dead. My guess is that it's one of those psychopaths you hear about, a schizo, a serial killer. The sort of monster that likes to kill people one by one. Likes to get them alone, get 'em scared, then turn the screw on 'em until they can't take it no more, and then...oh yes, then, it comes out of the darkness and shows 'em what's under its skin which is everything they've ever been scared of, all the crawling, yellow-eyed nightmares from their childhood—the boogeyman and the stranger, the breathing thing in the closet and the monster under the bed. Right before it strikes, oooo-weee-oooo, it scares 'em so bad their fucking heart stops and—"

"WHO THE HELL IS THIS?" Dew demanded.

For a few seconds there was nothing but more crackling over the radio, only this time it seemed to have a sort of rhythm to it. *"C'mon, Twelve. What fun would that be? You're a cop, you figure it out. But you better figure quick because I got your two boys in my sights and I'm going to stuff myself with their guts and chew on their livers unless you stop me. Then I'm going to come for you same as I came for each and every one at the mine."*

Dew tried to maintain his composure. "You think it's just the three of us? Guess again. There's an army of cops behind us and they'll keep coming for you."

The voice giggled like a child now. *"No they won't, Dew. You know why? Because your time and my time are not real time. See, you only left to come here ten minutes ago and in an hour from now, you won't even be gone yet. By the time you're dead, my friend, it'll be yesterday."*

Dew tried to make sense of that, but it was baffling. "Why don't you just quit hiding and we'll discuss this man to man. How about that?"

"Again, what fun would that be? Where's the challenge? Where's the contest of wills? No, I don't think that'll work at all." There was silence for a moment, silence punctuated by the humming of the voice. *"You don't have much time. I'm getting powerful hungry and when I fill myself, then the fun really starts. What do you think about that, Diddly-Dew with the cowshit on your shoe? How does that grab you? This is my place and my time and nobody gets out alive..."*

27

Dew was shaking.

From head to foot, he was shaking. He'd never known fear like this, sheer terror that was physically incapacitating. He was afraid to move and afraid not to. He could feel things moving around him in the dark and he had to suppress the very real need to scream like a little girl. *What do you think about that, Diddly-Dew with the cowshit on your shoe?* That's what the voice had said, but there was no way it could know, not about Diddly-Dew which is what Dew's Uncle Jake had called him as a kid. But the voice couldn't know that and it couldn't know about the time he stepped right up to his ankle in a cow flop and Uncle Jake had roared with laughter. *Jesus H. Christ, if you ain't Diddly-Dew with the cowshit on your shoe!* The voice couldn't know that. Nobody alive remembered any of that, but that voice, it knew…it *knew*…

Dew scrambled down the ladder off the dump truck.

He was driven by fear and by anger. He hit the ground running. If this was Twelve then Three would be right down the row. Yes, he saw as he ran, they were all lined up according to number. And there was three. As he ran towards it, its headlights came on, blinding him momentarily. Around the front and to the ladder. Gun in hand, he climbed up it, as scared as he'd ever been but pissed-off, too. Needing to vent, needing to take it all out on somebody, anybody.

There was no one in the cab.

No, he realized, with a sinking feeling in his guts, that wasn't necessarily true. There was nobody, but there was something. On the seat in a sticky pool of drying blood there was a severed human hand gripping the radio mic. A stink of bad meat came off it which was quickly replaced by something like peppermints.

Dew stared at it, cold fingers walking up his spine.

He was certain that if he didn't get the hell out of there and get out of there right now, that hand was going to move like in an old movie. It was going to crawl across the seat and fasten itself to his throat.

The peppermint odor became stronger until it was gagging, like trying to draw a breath through a sack of peppermint patties.

Numbly, feeling drained and beaten, he fumbled his way down the steps. He had to go find Jerry and Woody. He'd been down here some time now, giving that monster a chance to get at them, and he had to wonder why he'd waited so long playing this game. Had it been his idea or something planted in his head?

The smell. Think about the smell. It's related and you know it.

He started across the garage bay, moving faster and faster, certain something was behind him. That when he reached out for the door it would reach out for him,too, and yank him back.

But that didn't happen.

The lights went out instead.

6

Woody started toward the partially open door and Jerry grabbed him, put his hands on him. "No," he said. "No, we're not going in there...somebody wants us to and that's why we're not going to."

Woody shrugged him off. "We're cops. We have to." He said this in a low, barely audible voice. "C'mon."

"Wait," Jerry said. "The clock. Look at the fucking clock!"

Woody didn't like the idea of taking his eyes off the door and what might be behind it, but he did. And if for no other reason than to placate his partner. "It's a clock. So what?"

"Look at the time."

Now he was getting it.

As the realization sunk in, it felt like the wind had leaked out of him and he had all he could do to stay on his feet. It was just your basic office wall clock, white face with large black numbers. It read 7:35. Which was insane because it had to be after eleven by now. At 7:30, Jerry and he had still been on patrol. Dew had not yanked them for this little spook hunt yet.

He opened his mouth to say that the clock had stopped, but he could clearly see the seconds hand moving. It was still running. But if it was 7:30, then none of this had even happened yet. Dew had said the cell phone in the Mess Hall had been texting at quarter after eight, which was easily three hours ago.

What the hell was going on?

As he stood there, faced by the clock and what might be behind the door, the absence of Dew and Jerry's pale, frightened face, it felt like his mind was ready to fly apart, to exit his head and blow away like wheat chaff scattered on the wind.

"It's just a clock, Jerry. It probably don't work, needs its battery changed or something," he said, not believing it for a moment and completely ignoring the black power cord that dangled from it and was clearly plugged into a wall socket.

Jerry nodded. He knew it was bullshit, too. He recognized wild leaps of logic when he heard them just as he recognized

Woody's futile attempts at making sense of things. But he was desperate for anything, any sort of glue that would hold his world together. He was like a scared little kid who needed to be told everything would be all right.

Gun in hand, Woody approached the door.

It was open maybe a foot, a thick, murky darkness beyond it. That darkness could have held just about anything. He told himself it was just a man, some whacko playing head games and when he got his hands on that sonofabitch, boy, was he was going to be one sorry prick. *Just an ordinary man...that's what you think? An ordinary man that can be banging the walls and be in this room and outside the outer door? You heard it screech when Jerry fired through the door. No human being could sound like that.* Woody ignored that voice because he didn't believe in spooks. Or, at least, at that moment that's what he kept telling himself.

He was tense inside, his muscles bunched, every tendon drawn tight, every nerve ending jangling. He motioned to Jerry behind him that he was going to kick the door in all the way. Jerry nodded.

Swallowing, Woody brought his foot up.

The door slammed shut.

He jumped back and Jerry made a sort of *"Uhhhh,"* grunting noise as if he had been socked in the belly.

Woody was sweating now, his face beaded in perspiration. He could taste the salt on his lips when he licked them. *Okay, okay.* He stood his ground even as Jerry had shrank back.

"You in there! Open that goddamned door right now and show yourself!" he cried. "This is a police officer ordering you to come out of there!"

Which sounded good except there was no reply...except a sort of sobbing noise that was so quiet he wasn't sure if he had heard it at all.

Jerry made a gasping sound as a fist on the other side of the door drummed repeatedly.

Enough. Enough of this shit.

Woody stepped over there, his heart pounding in his temples. He was terrified, but he wasn't going to give in. It had never been as important to stand up as it was right now. He was going in there. That's how Dew would have handled it so he would follow suit. When got there, the knocking stopped.

Okay.

He gripped the knob. The door was open. He pushed it in two or three inches and a hot reek of blood came out of there again. It was repulsive. He was reminded of traffic fatalities he'd been in on. When people died violently, trapped in a mangled coffin of steel and shattered glass, this is what the inside of their cars smelled like. Once, out on Highway 10, he recalled, a little Dodge Neon had run a stop sign and been broadsided by a pulp truck loaded with logs. It had dragged the Neon seventy feet. By the time they arrived on scene, it looked like a giant had crushed it like a beer can. Woody and Pete Monroe (since retired), had wrenched the door open to get at the injured inside even though they knew there was no way they could have survived trauma like that. When the door opened, blood had run out of the car in copious amounts, right over the tips of Woody's shiny black duty boots.

And it had smelled like what was coming out of the room before him.

Nausea bubbling in his stomach, he moved fast and kicked the door open, gun in one hand, tactical flashlight in the other.

In the jiggling light beam, he saw another office with file cabinets against the wall, a desk and a computer…and someone sitting in the chair behind it.

By then, Jerry had found the light switch.

"He's dead," Jerry said.

And Woody wanted to say, *no shit, you think?*

The guy behind the desk was middle-aged with a bristly silver-gray crewcut, a white dress shirt and tie. There was a tattoo of a fish on his right forearm. His hands were curled up like claws in his lap. His body was arched in the chair, his head thrown back, mouth wide in agony. He appeared to have died in great pain and Woody did not doubt that because there was a hatchet buried in his skull, brain matter and blood slopped down his face.

It was grisly, but as much as he was sickened, he realized there was something very wrong here.

Jerry refused to look at the cadaver. "Let's…let's just go get Dew, okay? C'mon, Woody, *please.*"

"Just wait," Woody said.

He walked around the desk and prodded the body with the end of his flashlight. It did not give. He tapped it against the corpse's arm. *Thump, thump.* It was hard as a rock. Whoever this guy was, he was frozen like a steak in a deep freeze. There was frost on his bare arms and on his face. The blood looked crystallized.

"He's hard as a rock," Woody said.

Jerry made a gasping sound. "That's insane, man. It's forty-odd degrees out there and it's gotta be closer to seventy in here. Woody, it can't be. Do you hear me? *It can't fucking be.*"

But it was.

This guy had been killed by the hatchet blow—and, Jesus, the blade was buried over three inches into the crown of his skull—and then frozen, put back in this chair to thaw. There was no other door leading out. How had they gotten him in here? And better yet, who had knocked and slammed the door?

There was absolutely nowhere to hide.

Woody again felt like his mind was splitting its seams. How did you explain this? How did you even begin to make sense of a clusterfuck like this?

On the screen of the desktop computer, there was a bloody handprint…except whoever had left it must have been quite unusual. There was only the print of a knobby sort of thumb and three long fingers. A four-fingered hand? It was inconceivable. Besides, the way it was shaped. It almost looked more like the print of a bird's foot.

"C'mon, Woody, let's go."

Woody nodded. That's what they needed to do, all right. This mess was for the State Patrol's CSI people. Let them figure out the hows and whys. Still, he stood there, staring at the corpse, imprinting it upon his brain for future nightmares, listening to it drip as it began to thaw.

Drip.

Drip.
Drip...

7

The State Patrol were roughly an hour behind Dew and his people. They started the climb up the winding road high above Mineral City, the headlights of their SUV splashing over the muddy road and its great melting blobs of snow. Trooper Jay Nagle was driving, Trooper Tanya Seatin riding shotgun. As they followed the winding road through great stands of dark forest, the mine workings rising high above them like the battlements of a castle, Tanya was saying, "My biggest problem with white people is that they won't tell the truth."

"Oh Christ, here we go again," Jay said.

"None of you will say how you *really* feel."

"You're making generalizations," he told her.

"I don't think so. You say you don't like our president. Great. I say he's okay, far better than the oil baron we had before him who started two wars that accomplished absolutely nothing. I openly admit why I didn't like that guy, but you won't admit why you don't like *this* guy."

"It's his policies."

She laughed. "Really? *Really?* See, that right there is my problem with white people. You guys know you don't like him because he's black but you don't have the balls to admit it. You hide behind rhetoric and political correctness. You're afraid of being called racist even though most of you are."

"You know I'm not like that," Jay said.

"No, I know you're *exactly* like that." Tanya was staring at him now. She had him on the ropes and she was not going to let him up. "You and the rest of these brain-washed idiots who swallow every ounce of propaganda Fox News shoves down their throats. And don't look at me like that. You know I'm right. You know I'm speaking the truth. Now why don't you try it?"

Her voice, her damnable voice. God, it seemed so much louder in his head, echoing and echoing, gaining volume and force until he wanted to scream.

"Enough, okay?" he said.

She shook her head. "If you recall, you were one of these people that believed in the birther nonsense."

"I did not."

"Yes, you did, Jay. You and I argued about it."

He sighed. "Okay, I admit I was wrong."

"Great, now admit the rest of it."

She was baiting him and he knew it. He had to maintain control, he could not rise to the surface. The more she talked, the more it felt like there was an itching in the back of his head, a terrible scratching that did not belong.

"C'mon, Jay, just say it. Say what's on your mind."

I won't! I won't! I can't speak the truth because I don't have black skin to hide behind! Any time white people speak the truth they're racists and any time they stand up for their own cultural identity or take pride in who and what they are, minorities scream that they're the KKK and Nazis and all that other shopworn crapola—

Inwardly, Jay ground his teeth. God, it was close that time. That damn Tanya, she just loved pushing his buttons. Anytime they were alone like this, she went after him. She got off on it. She found her token right-wing target and she wasn't going to stop until she drew blood. He knew right away when they got the call to go up to the mine that she was going to go after him.

"What do you want me to admit?" he said, trying to maintain control even though he wanted to say some things she wouldn't like.

"The truth."

"I don't like his policies."

"And that's because…"

"Because I don't."

"Come on, Jay."

God, he wanted to slap her right across the face. The scratching in his head was louder than ever. It sounded like a dozen fingers were scraping against the inside of his skull. "Jesus H. Christ, Tanya. What do you want from me? You want me to say I don't like black people? That's not true. I like you just fine…when you're not hounding me."

Jay bit his tongue at that point because he knew he would say some bad things if he did not. There were voices in his head and they were screaming at him. They wanted him to tell the truth, to finally admit the truth. That hip-hop and rap were not even music and how nobody should be paid millions of dollars to run around on a field with a ball in their hands or to throw it into a hoop and that somebody should take Al Sharpton and shove him up Jesse Jackson's ass and put both of them in a hole with Malcolm goddamn X and Martin Luther King. Because civil rights and the NAACP were a sham, a shadow play, and the only reason white people were trying to treat blacks like equals was because of their overwhelming guilt which was probably misplaced—

"I'm glad you like me, Jay. I really am," she said. "But have you noticed our president? Shit, somebody turns out the lights and that dude is all eyes and teeth."

"Stop it." *She's asking for it. She's really, honestly asking for it.*

"You know I won't. Not until you admit a few things."

"I will not admit that stuff."

She laughed. "Man, getting white people to admit to the truth is harder than finding a good ham sandwich in Tel Aviv."

"Huh?"

"Skip it."

He felt his face getting hot. The blood in his veins had been replaced by steam. "Skip *what?* You're always saying shit and throwing things at me that I don't understand and you're doing it so you can feel fucking superior to me."

"Jay, c'mon, take it easy."

But he couldn't. He seemed to have no control over it. "No, I'm not taking it fucking easy. Why don't you quit that uppity, self-fucking-important black woman shit already? You're not better than me. You're not better than anyone."

"Jay...stop it. Please. You're getting irrational."

"Fuck you."

"Jay…"

What the hell was happening? It was like a can of something ugly had been opened up inside him and he wanted to shake it all over her. He wanted to hurt her. He wanted to wrap his fingers around her throat and thumb her eyeballs out. Better, he wanted to reduce her to the level where he thought she belonged. *But I don't think that! I don't! I like Tanya! She's okay! She's just got a big fucking mouth!* But what was inside him didn't want to hear that whitey apologist bullshit; it wasn't true. This bitch had been badgering him for months, goddamn years, it seemed. She was going to get what she was begging for. He was going to show her—

"Jay? *Jay?"* Tanya said and her voice held real concern. "Are you all right?"

He suddenly wasn't sure. It was as if his brain had been hijacked, made to think things it did not want to think. His teeth were clenched and his chin was shiny with drool. He wiped it away with the back of his fist. He made himself calm down. "Sure…yeah, I'm fine."

Now Tanya was watching him very closely.

He could feel her dark eyes boring into him. She was not superior now; she was scared. She knew she had crossed the line. And he wanted to say, *no, no, Tanya, you know I'd never hurt you. It's just this place…it…it's getting under my skin and in my head.* But he didn't. Even when he tried to, the words would not come.

He was grateful when he saw the gates of Superior Mining which meant they had arrived on-scene and Tanya wouldn't be able to turn up the heat any higher until it became an all-out race war between them. *One that coon bitch will not survive.* No, no, no, he didn't think that. It wasn't him, it was someone else.

Stop it, you gotta stop this shit.

He pulled the SUV through the gates and paused at the guard shack. It was dark. It was obvious no one was around.

"That's funny," Tanya said. "You think somebody would be at the gate." She grabbed the radio mic, but she couldn't get anything. Nothing but static and a whining background noise. "Must be in some kind of dead zone up here."

"Sure," Jay said.

The road split ahead. According to the signs, the left fork led to the mine itself, the Empire Pit, while the right led to the offices. He turned to the right, the SUV splashing through puddles. The wipers were clearing droplets of rain from the windshield as the headlights peeled back the night, exposing dark outbuildings and equipment yards, crawling shadows that fluttered around the vehicle like black curtains.

"Sure is quiet up here," Tanya said, still watching him.

And it was. It seemed like they should have seen some sign of life by now. The entire complex had a very dead feeling to it that he didn't like at all. He figured it was mostly imagination. Thinking this calmed him somewhat.

When dispatch sent them up to Superior, they weren't told about the 911 call that made Dew and his deputies scramble up here. They were only told of a possible civil disturbance and that was a good thing. They didn't need anything more to fuel their imaginations because there was already enough wood for the fire.

"Lights ahead," Tanya said.

Jay nodded. A couple more turns of the road and they'd be there. He thought it couldn't come quickly enough. The night, the falling rain, that ominous feeling of emptiness up here…it was getting to him. It was beginning to feel like his spine wanted to roll up. He tried to keep it in check. He had been afraid before, but never like this. It was building in him and as it did, he gripped the steering wheel that much tighter. The only truly good thing was that scratching in his head, that hating voice, was gone now.

He saw a large parking lot. It seemed to go on forever, lot after lot after lot. Beyond them, there was a maze of buildings, tall and short, three-story brick and sheet metal prefab all bunched together. Above them, he could see the old mine works crouching on the hills—head frames and hoist shacks. In the rain and mist they looked like dinosaurs coming out of the night.

"Wait," he said.

"What?"

He blinked his eyes and blinked them again. A shiver ran from his scalp down to his balls. "I thought…I thought I saw the sheriff's cruiser parked up by the offices."

"I don't see anything," Tanya told him.

Jay didn't either. And that was the crazy thing because he was certain it had been sitting right there in front, but as he came around a parked row of pickups it was gone as if it had never been there.

But I saw it. It was sitting right there. I saw the bubbles on top.

"You okay, Jay?" Tanya asked.

"Sure, except I'm imagining shit."

"So am I," she admitted. "I thought I saw someone standing there under the light, waving to us."

Jay, feeling more than a little uneasy, brought the SUV around until the lights were pointed directly at the offices. There was no one there.

"We better take a look," he said. "All these vehicles out here, there's gotta be someone around."

"Sure."

He pulled to a stop, idling. Neither of them moved. It was as if finding those other people is what scared them most.

8

Dew went still as a park statue as the lights went out.

They didn't go out all at once as you might expect, but dimmed gradually until he was lost in a field of utter blackness. The last thing to go out were the glaring headlights of Number Three dump truck. They winked out like the eyes of an ogre, leaving him in a womb of blackness that seemed darker than anything he had ever known before.

His heart pumping madly in his chest, his breath scraping in his lungs, Dew knew he had to keep his cool here. If he panicked, all was lost. He reached down to his Sam Browne and unclipped the tactical flashlight. He realized he still had his gun in his hand. He slid it back in its holster and pulled out his fiberglass baton.

Now we'll see who wants to fucking dance, he thought.

Step by step, he moved towards the door because that's where he had been going when the lights went out. It was ten feet away and no more. He kept walking, the darkness feeling alive around him with moving shapes. They were there. He knew they were there. It was all about nerve now. Whatever was doing this, it was trying to squeeze the stuffing out of him with anxiety. He had to keep his head. It was all he really had now.

He toyed with the idea of turning on his flashlight, but despite the fear that gripped him, he would not. That's exactly what they wanted him to do so they could show him things that would strip his mental gears. He refused. He'd use it, all right, but not just yet.

You do nothing else, a voice in his head told him, *you make goddamn sure those two kids are okay.*

Kids. Jesus. Jerry and Woody were both nearly thirty, yet he felt protective of them like they were both schoolboys. But that's how it got when you were a grizzled, old school cop like Dew LeBay who would be seeing sixty in three years. Anyone who hadn't seen forty was a snot-nosed, green kid who needed his ass wiped on a regular basis—

Where the fuck was that door?

Dew trusted his sense of orientation, even here in the dark, and he knew damn well that he had walked in a straight line. He should have found the door by now.

Where the hell was it?

Something passed close by his left ear with an odd, metallic buzzing. It was no fly, no bug. He knew that much. Something brushed his shoulder and he swung the baton in its direction without contacting anything but dead air.

He couldn't take any more of this shit.

He turned on the flashlight.

What the fuck?

He saw in an instant that he wasn't even walking towards the door. No, somehow, someway, he had been completely turned around. He had done a full 360° and was walking down the center of the garage bay. He knew it wasn't possible. If he hadn't have known better, he would have thought that it was not he who changed direction but the entire goddamn garage.

"So you like your games, do you?" he said under his breath, needing to hear his own voice.

Okay.

All right.

That was fine.

He saw where the door was and headed right towards it. The light was directed at it now and nothing was going to screw him up this time. Nothing. He was within feet of it when something hit him in the back, knocking him forward, then something else punched into his side, making him cry out. He swung the baton and, again, there was nothing. He whirled around and something hit his hand, the flashlight spinning from his grip. He went for it and something warm and flabby attached itself to the back of his neck.

He screamed.

He couldn't help himself.

The thing grabbed him with a soft, flaccid mouth that felt like huge fleshy lips and he could feel a ring of tiny, needling teeth digging into the nape of his neck. He reached back and tore at something huge and segmented like a flying centipede but it only gripped that much tighter. It held on not only with its mouth, but with two limbs that gripped his head tightly and were spiked like the flesh of a cactus.

With a burst of fury and revulsion, he threw himself backwards, crushing the thing between himself and the door. It let go, its mouth making a popping sound as suction was broken, the spiky limbs that gripped his head tearing out mats of hair from his scalp.

But there were others.

He could hear them circling out there with that same horrible buzzing sound which sounded like dozens and dozens of sharp pins scraping over sheet metal. It went right up his spine. He had his gun out by then and fired twice in the direction of the buzzing. Whether he hit anything or not, he didn't know.

The door was behind him, but he had to have that damn flashlight.

It was a matter of life and death now.

Do it for chrissake.

He holstered his weapon, jumped forward, landing hard on his belly, the wind nearly knocked out of him. He scrambled forward, fingers finding the flashlight and gripping it as more of the insects—or whatever in the hell they were—swooped down at him like moths around a streetlight. He crab-crawled back towards the door and pulled himself to his feet.

One of the bugs flew within inches of his face, another lunged at him with a sound not unlike a World War II dive bomber coming in fast and low to deliver its payload. It came rocketing out of the darkness and he swung the baton at it. It splattered as he hit it, as if it was made of some sort of jelly.

Enough.

Christ, there had to be dozens of them out there.

But were they really there or only in his mind? He was not exactly sure. His brain was trying to think, trying to reason, trying to make some earthly sense of this but all it was succeeding in doing was tripping over its own logic.

He slid the baton into his belt, holding the flashlight out before him in a trembling fist, he reached behind him and clutched the doorknob. At that very moment, one of the insects appeared at the very outer edge of the light beam. It hovered there like a hummingbird outside a window, making that tinny, scratching, buzzing sort of noise. He had never seen anything like it. It was an insect from a nightmare. It was well over three feet in length, sort of a dusty gray with rust-colored flecks, its body long, streamlined, and segmented (just as his fingers had told him). The segments were rounded and flared out at the sides into some sort of rudimentary wings that were diaphanous and fluttering like the swimmerets of a shrimp. This was how it flew and hovered. It had a pair of immense, hooked grasping claws that resembled ant mandibles, a set of glossy pink eyes at the end of fibrous stalks, and a circular mouth big around as the opening of a coffee can that was ringed with sharp yellow teeth. The mouth was constantly pulsating as if it wanted very badly to grab onto something.

Dew could see five or six others hovering just behind it, all of them anxious to get at him.

He opened the door and right away, the lead bug came at him with a whining, buzzing sound and he shot at it and hit it. The 9mm round seemed to split it in half like a walnut shell and whatever happened after that, he did not know because he slammed the door shut on it.

He could hear them out there, scratching to get in.

He sank to his knees, biting down on his knuckles to stop the madness from encroaching any farther into his thoughts. He had to hold it together. He had to. All he had now was the thing his enemies had always feared most: his dogged tenacity. He had never given up before and he sure as hell would not give up now.

9

It began with a hissing and a popping.

Woody heard it as he turned to leave the secondary office and its awful occupant. The sound stopped him and Jerry simultaneously. It was not something you could turn away from and not in the sort of place they were in with its attendant weirdness.

"Hell's going on?" Jerry asked.

Woody just shook his head. The hissing sound reminded him of a documentary he'd once seen on the gas chamber where pellets of cyanide were dropped into a vat of sulfuric acid. They made the same sort of hissing sound he was hearing now.

The corpse behind the desk was steaming.

The dripping sound of slow defrosting he'd heard only moments before was accelerated now. Not a dripping, but a splattering like slush falling from a roof during a midwinter thaw. The corpse seemed to be shrinking in the chair and that was because—as they watched with mouths hanging so wide open they might have been hinged—it was dissolving like tablets of Alka-Seltzer in a glass of water.

"It's...it's *melting,*" Jerry said in a dry voice.

And it was.

That was the perfectly insane part about it all.

Not just thawing like a frozen pork chop on a kitchen counter, but *melting,* going to slop and slime and mush. The stench was unbelievable, like a cauldron of boiling blood and marrow fat. The steam from the corpse gathered in a thick, wet haze in the air. Things fell. Things plopped and splatted. As it went on, the process seemed to accelerate, the body hissing and thumping in the chair, fluids gushing from it and jellied sections of tissue falling free like sheets of ice.

"Oh God," Jerry said through a mouthful of warm saliva. "Oh Jesus."

How long would something like this take? Woody wondered. *How long?*

Even in the heat of the room, which couldn't have been much more than sixty-eight or seventy, it would have taken days for something frozen as solid as the corpse to thaw. It would have been a painfully slow process. It would not have happened this fast. The cadaver would not have...*liquefied.*

Yet, that's exactly what it was doing.

The face slopped off the red, grinning skull beneath. There was a popping noise (that sounded a little too much like somebody drawing their finger along the inside of their cheek) and the corpse's left eye blew from its socket. Trailing its optic nerve, it rolled over the desk blotter.

Jerry gasped and ran into the other room.

Woody could hear him vomiting into the same wastepaper can he'd kicked over in frustration not that long before. By that point, Woody was slouched in the doorway, gasping at the stink rolling from the corpse in its rapid dissolution. He had no idea what sort of toxic fumes were coming off the remains. He should have gotten out of there, but he simply could not stop watching it. It was like seeing a wax dummy melting. The flesh was not just oozing free, but seeming to boil from it like hot tallow in ribbons and mucid strings. And as that happened, the skeleton beneath was revealed—a gape-jawed Halloween horror with a hatchet firmly planted in its skull.

He couldn't take it anymore.

He staggered from the doorway and dropped to one knee like a man that had been gassed. He coughed and gagged, his head spinning. He could hear Jerry still retching and gagging, making a perfectly repulsive gobbling sort of sound as he tried to clear the bile from his throat. Woody wasn't sure which was worse: the smell of the corpse or the stink of hot puke.

Then Jerry was coughing and spitting. "Woody!" he cried. "It's...it's Dew!"

Dew? Is that what he said?

That word had the same effect on him as a sunny afternoon or a weekend off. Something inside of him jumped for joy. It did cartwheels and handsprings. It wanted to sing and dance and shout. Dew. Fucking Dew. That crusty, tough SOB would know what to do. It didn't matter how perfectly crazy all this was, Dew would know exactly how to handle it because guys like Dew always did.

Woody climbed to his feet.

He ignored the hollow sort of crashing he heard from the other office because he knew it was just a rack of bones sliding out of a chair and hitting the floor. What of it? There were worse things than skeletons. Far worse things.

Jerry, wiping his mouth, was standing before the window, pointing. Woody saw, all right. There was Dew, that loveable hard-assed nut-buster, standing down in the garage waving at them. They both waved back and he motioned them down. This was it. This whole freakishly fucked-up affair was at an end, praise Jesus.

"Let's go!" Jerry said, practically wagging his tail like a puppy.

"Sure," Woody said.

But for one moment, he hesitated because he saw something strange. But it was nothing. It couldn't be anything. Just an optical illusion, a trick of the eye. Yet, for one second there he thought he'd seen Dew's image waver like a candle flame.

But that was ridiculous.

Feeling relieved and yet concerned, he followed Jerry out to the ramp that led below.

10

Getting out of the SUV seemed to be the hardest part of all. Tanya stood there before the office door with her flashlight in hand, staring at the gold leaf on the plate glass which announced the hours of operation. She had the worst feeling of dread in the back of her mind but she could not encapsulate it and make sense of it. It was just there, brooding and intense, making her belly feel fluttery down low. She didn't like it. She wasn't sure whether what she feared was in front of her—inside the building—or behind her—Jay. There was something funny with him tonight. Usually, they argued things like politics and race back and forth. It was their thing.

But not tonight.

Tonight he was edgy and strange, almost threatening. She had the worst feeling back there that he wanted to kill her. That he had the strongest desire to pull his piece and cap a few into her.

Now you're being ridiculous.

But no, she honestly didn't think so.

She could feel him standing behind her and it made her nervous. It was as if it was not Jay at all but someone else, someone dangerous, an escaped lunatic in a bad horror movie. *Nuts. You're plain old nuts.* And maybe she was, but she could not convince herself that she was wrong.

"Nice to get some fresh air anyway," she said to him, breathing in and out. "It was getting stifling in there."

He grunted. "I liked it. Kind of chilly out here."

Tanya cocked her head. "You think so? Seemed hot in there. Like a fucking greenhouse, man. I was sweating in my African skin, five generations removed."

He said nothing.

She didn't like it. Usually things like that made him laugh. Those were two things she'd always been good at with him: pissing him off and making him laugh. Apparently, she was still good at the one but not the other. She was going to mention the pine tree air freshener in the cruiser, how it stank so bad she felt like she was doing the backstroke in a bottle of Pine-Sol, how she'd had the strongest desire to pick pine needles out of her teeth…but, no, humor was lost on him tonight. Still, it had been weirdly piney in the cruiser. The smell so sharp it was practically nauseating.

She tried the door. It was locked.

"What now?" she said. "Radio's out. Place is locked up. This is all probably a practical joke."

Jay ignored her.

That was strange in of itself. Usually when they were in situations like this, he had a tendency to stand a little too close to her, to brush up against her for no reason. Now Tanya realized— as her grandma had told her again and again—that she wasn't as smart as an owl in a tree, but every woman knew what that meant. Jay was divorced, but she was married. Happily, she liked to think. Yet, the idea of being with him had occurred to her more often than she liked to admit. He was a big guy, strong, muscular. He was an ex-Marine and he was still built like one. She was small and petite save for her ass which was probably a little too big. She was chesty, though, and she'd caught him scrutinizing her goods more than once. Sometimes it made her uncomfortable, sometimes it made her burn. And that was why him ignoring her bothered her in ways she could not exactly fathom.

She could hear her grandma now. *Bad enough that you married a white man, but to think of cheating on him with another white man. Girl, you're asking for trouble. They got trees in Wisconsin so I hear. And you gonna find your black ass hanging from one of them if you don't watch out.* But that was Grandma Ruby. She was racist because she'd been raised racist. She only had two rules in life—the first was that you minded your own business and the second was that you married within your own race. *I don't hate white folk,* she'd said more than once. *But I steer clear of 'em. If their eyes were knives, I would have bled to death a hundred times by now.* Ruby was down in a senior care center outside Cincinnati now. Her mind was nearly gone. Tanya wondered why she was thinking about her and about Jay in that way…but still, maybe some morning they'd go out for coffee and then—

"Door's open," Jay said.

"It was locked."

"Well, it's not locked now, you dumb black twat."

Tanya froze in place. *What the hell did you say?"*

Jay looked at her. "I said it's not locked now."

"You said something else, Jay."

"No, I didn't."

"You called me a dumb black twat."

He just stood there. "What the hell are you talking about? I said no such thing."

But he had, she knew he had. Yet…his demeanor was rock solid. In fact, he looked wronged as if she had accused him of something unthinkable. She was about to go after him full bore…but now she wasn't so sure. It seemed, as she thought about it, that maybe that last part had echoed only in her mind.

"Are you okay?" he asked.

No, I'm far from okay. "Yeah, I…uh…I thought you mumbled something."

"I wouldn't do that, Tanya."

He turned from her and pulled the door open. It was certainly not locked. She wondered if it was some kind of trick. Something angry in her had the feeling that he thought she was just a dumb woman and maybe a dumb *black* woman to boot, maybe even a *dumb black twat*. Again, she nearly said something, but then she stepped into the offices of Superior Mining and a chill went right up her spine.

"You smell that?" she said instead.

"I don't smell anything. Just your perfume."

"Jay, I'm not wearing any perfume."

He didn't comment on that. So he *was* smelling it then: that pervasive, overpowering sweet smell. It was cloying and thick in the air.

"Let's take a quick look," he said. "Then we'll get out of here, down out of these hills where the radio will work."

She didn't bother pointing out that her cell had gone toes up, too. No sense complicating matters. She followed him through the reception area and to a doorway beyond. It was open and they stepped through. Right away, that sweet smell hit her with force and stopped her dead.

"You all right?" he asked.

"No...that smell. God."

"I don't smell anything."

She didn't believe that for a moment, but then, as she followed him farther into the room beyond, the smell dissipated until it was simply no more which made no sense whatsoever. She was sweating now. Her perspiration had a distinctive sour odor to it which was the smell of fear oozing out of her pores and she knew it. She was terrified of this place, but she couldn't understand exactly why. The smell was part of it, but only part of it. She felt that she was very close to screaming...only there really was nothing to scream about.

Jay was a few feet in front of her. He had his flashlight out and he was scanning the room. It was a big room and she expected to see desks lined up, computers idling, bulletin boards, and filing cabinets, perhaps a water bubbler in the corner somewhere.

But that isn't what Jay's light revealed nor her own.

Am I losing it? Am I cracking up?

She saw that, yes, the room was large, very large, and could have held thirty desks comfortably...but it did not hold desks. Everything was filthy, covered in a fine deep pile of accumulated grime. The air was murky with a yellow-brown haze, specules of dust spinning and drifting like the silt in a sunken ship. To the left there was an intricate series of shelves holding compartments large and small. All of them were heaped with yellowed bones or had jawless human skulls lined up in them. It looked like the set for a walk-through haunted house. She saw other things like cabinets—or perhaps *caskets*—set upright against the walls, lids nailed shut or partially open. There were clusters of what looked like mummified birds hanging from the ceiling, corkboards set with huge, alien-looking insects pinned to them—leggy things like huge beetles and mutant crickets and arachnids from another dimension with jeweled red eyes set on quivering stems. The birds, some of them at least, were still trying to flutter their wings. She saw a crowded display of what looked like tribal fetish masks, some carved sad-looking, some wicked, and others decidedly evil...except they weren't masks, but faces, death-masks that were hideously alive, muscles flexing, lips smacking and mouths pulling into grins.

Tanya felt terror, real unbridled terror that was white-hot like liquid pig iron, burn through her. Her mouth made gasping sounds and her eyes would not blink. Her hand was shaking so badly that the light jumped on the walls, making objects seem to creep and dance.

As Jay's light illuminated the other wall, she saw it held a profusion of large jars and bottles and glass vats, all of them stoppered and crowding for space. And all of them filled with cloudy plasma and discolored serums in which fleshy objects drifted. It was like a pickled punk collection from a sideshow, deformed and misshapen babies and freaks of nature. Bloated white fetuses with too many limbs or clearly not enough. Two heads or none at all. Semi-human and patently *non*-human laboratory specimens that looked more like worms or spiders, monkeys or snakes, or nameless things that could not be described by a sane mind. She saw eyes watching her and puckered fingers tapping.

"Not much in here," Jay said.

"What? What?" she wailed, something in her mind cracking open like a peanut shell. *"What do you fucking mean there's not much in here?"*

He was walking amongst it all and she was trembling inside her own skin because she felt things moving around her, splintered fingernails scraping over the walls and blobby forms inching sluglike over the floors. *But Jay was oblivious to it all.* That was the amazing part. She was so afraid that it seemed like she was shrinking, becoming smaller, a diminutive creature that could have crawled through a mouse hole in the wall.

"Now this is funny," he said, aiming his flashlight at a poster on the wall. "What they don't think of."

Brushing drifting cobwebs from her face, she looked at it closer. What she saw was just as insane as everything else in this fucking menagerie. It was like something from an old-time traveling carnival, yellowing and wrinkled, the corners rolling up. There was a black-and-white illustration of a dancing two-headed skeleton. On a leash it held a rat with a distorted human face. Beneath that it read:

THE HORROR CHAMBER
of
PROFESSOR PARASITIUS

MIDNIGHT SPOOK SHOW!
TWICE THE THRILLS!
TWICE THE CHILLS!
ONE SOLID NIGHT OF GUT-RIPPING BLOOD HORRORS!

THE TOAD BOY* THE CRAWLING THING*
THE MELTING MAN*OLD SLIME FACE
SEE A GIANT ARACHNID SHED ITS SKIN!
SEE ALIEN NECK SUCKERS AND BULGE EYE!
WATCH DWIGHT ROSE DEFILE A CORPSE!
SEE THE DUMB BLACK TWAT ROASTED IN HER OWN JUICES!

AND LIVE IN PERSON RIGHT ABOVE YOUR HEAD
THE SPIDER FROM MARS!!!
THE ONLY SHOW LIKE IT ON EARTH!
NO ONE GETS OUT ALIVE!
BE THERE AND BE SCARED!

Tanya stood there, stunned and nearly mindless, all of it rolling through her brain. *The dumb black twat roasted in her own juices.* It said it. Right there. On that poster that looked like it was eighty years old if it was a day. Jay was looking at her as if she was out of her head and maybe she was at that. She kept thinking: *And live in person right above your head the Spider from Mars.* She did not want to look up and see it, because she knew it was there. She could sense it hovering above her, dangling there in its web, a leggy horror from beyond space and time. Something that could not be, but was. It exuded a honeyed sickening odor, its legs making creaking, chitinous noises. Something warm and brown spattered the back of her hand. Another drop plopped against her face and ran down her cheek like a tear.

Spider blood, a voice in her mind whispered. *That's what it is, you know. Spider blood. Spider goo. Spider bile.*

"Now where do you suppose they got something like that?" Jay said, pointing his flashlight beam above her.

Tanya stumbled back, bringing her own light up and, yes, there it was, an immense spider that, of course, was no spider at all. At least, not one from Earth. Maybe Mars, but more likely from the deranged depths of her subconscious mind where such things not only lived but bred in horrible numbers.

It was huge and bulbous, probably four feet across and six in length. Its body was a pulsating fleshy mass of brown tissue set with fine black spines. It had a variety of bony limbs that looked like winter-dead sticks, easily twelve or thirteen of them, far more than any garden-variety terrestrial spider. They made clicking sounds they tapped the silken strands of its gargantuan web. It had a sort of head that was skeletal and multi-chambered, set with a dozen eyes the size of golf balls. They were a feverish juicy pink like sores that were ready to burst. At the bottom of the head, there were two hooked chelicerae, jagged-edged and dripping venom. A variety of wiggling pedipalps were in constant motion.

But probably the most obscene thing about it was a long curling tongue that hung from its mouth like a coiling worm. It was so large she could see the taste buds on it. They were the size of nickels.

All that was bad enough.

It made Tanya's heart pound so fast she thought it would gallop itself to a stop. But what was worse and what almost finished her was that it spoke. In a voice like a needle scratching an old record, it said, *"Why, I figger I got me a nigger and I'm going to lick her and taste her until there ain't nothing left but fish bones and sputum! I'll suck her nipples off and lick her labia*

*to shreds and fuck the liver right out of that dumb black twat!
See if I don't!"*

That was it.

That was the breaking point.

She could take no more. She screamed with absolute hysteria and absolute volume. It was so loud Jay jumped back and almost went on his ass. If she could have directed it, she could have punched a hole right through the wall with it. As it was, it echoed through the room with a screeching, bone-numbing shrillness that even made the Spider from Mars pull back in its web and raise its venomous chelicerae in defense.

The scream had barely come cycling out of her when she drew her weapon—a Smith & Wesson blue-steel 9mm—and fired six rounds right into the spider that made it writhe and mewl like a stomped kitten.

Jay cried out, demanding to know what the hell she was doing but she wasn't sure herself. She only knew that that horror had to die and it had to die right fucking now.

The Spider from Mars was mewling and squeaking and making gurgling noises that just about brought Tanya's stomach into her throat. Its eyes were shuddering in their sockets and it seemed to be showing her faces, modeling its flesh like clay. The last one looked like the shrieking visage of her mother. Its hide was pulsing, splitting open and spilling a gray slime, a yellow architecture of exoskeleton trying to force itself free. It vomited out steaming gouts of brown juice that splattered over the floor.

But that was all Tanya saw because she turned and ran, knowing she could not watch anymore of it without losing what remained of her sanity.

11

By the time Dew made it up to the office, the lights were back on, but there was no one around. He saw that right away when he came through the door and wasn't it just like those two meatheads to disobey a direct order? He'd have their asses for this. He'd go up one side of them and down the other. He'd make sure they knew damn well who the captain of this fucking ship was.

But the smell...

That was what stopped him as he entered the room, that horrible stink in the air that wanted to put him to his knees. It was like warm vomit with something much stronger, much worse beyond it. If, at that moment, he'd had to identify it he would have said it stank like a deer camp at the end of season—a fusty, marrowy stench of hides and entrails, salty blood gathered in buckets and carcasses hung up to dry. Not a fresh odor, but a memory of slaughter and meat and pools of drainage on plank floors.

He didn't like it.

It made no sense, but nothing made much sense tonight. All he knew is that he was missing two deputies and if something had happened to them, it was going to tear his heart out by the red roots. Those two idiots were like sons to him. He knew their people. Woody's old man was a good friend and a retired cop himself. Dew could imagine the dread of having to tell those families face to face that their boys had died on his watch.

He shook that from his head because there was no time for such things. Maudlin thinking like that would weaken his resolve and he couldn't allow that. There was simply too much at stake here.

Way too much.

He stepped farther into the office, bathing in that blood stink now. He wanted to get out of there. He wanted to find Woody and Jerry and bid Superior Mining a hasty goodbye, leave this goddamned mess to the State Patrol...but he wasn't leaving. Not just yet. It wasn't in him to do so. He had never thought in all his long years that he was nosy or overly curious by nature, but once a problem presented itself, he just couldn't leave it alone; he had to run it to ground or he would never rest.

So, knowing he had to do this, he walked across the room, noticing that the wastepaper can on the floor was the source of the vomit and that there were papers scattered about that should have probably been on the desk. The door on the other side was partially open and he told himself it was probably just a storage closet or something. Which was bullshit and he recognized it as such for the foul, seeping blood odor was coming from behind that door and he damn well knew it.

All right, quit thinking and just do it.

When he was in range, his throat feeling as if it had tightened down to a pinhole, he nudged the door open with the toe of his boot. What he saw was horrible, of course, but he'd been in the business too long to flinch from human remains. He took it all in and cataloged it—the desk and the pile of bones behind it, that oozing collection of viscous matter which must have been tissue that was somehow superheated to liquid and was quickly coagulating now. How such a thing was possible, he did not know any more than he knew whether the hatchet imbedded in the skull was connected to this all in some tenuous way.

Figuring, he had done his duty, he turned and walked back into the outer office, refusing to give into the gag reflex that wanted to convulse his stomach.

He stepped outside, staring down the ramp at the shadows below. He was smelling something else now…what was it? *Piss? Are you smelling piss?* He was. Pungent, sharp-smelling urine. The sort a man puts out first thing in the morning. But this was beyond that. It was positively caustic like ammonia. The walls outside the office were glistening.

This had happened while he was in the office.

He would have smelled it before if it had been there and he certainly would have seen the wet walls.

That meant whatever did this was close by.

Swallowing, Dew tried his radio. "Jerry, Woody, if you're reading this, let me know."

He waited.

"Jesus Christ, answer me," he tried again.

The static coming from the Motorola was unbroken. He expected to hear some ear-splitting squeal erupt from it, but he didn't. He stood there, listening to the static. It sounded like dead air and nothing else. Earlier, though he'd dismissed it as imagination, he'd had the eerie feeling that the static was not simply static, but that there was something behind it, something listening. But now that feeling was gone. It probably meant nothing...*probably*. Either his mind was just running wild (it was) or whatever was here at the mine playing these awful tricks was gone. It had checked out or taken a break, was pushed back with its feet up, bladder duly emptied.

The very idea of that was silly.

But he was certain that whatever negative charge there had been in the air, that indefinable something, that malevolent presence, was gone. The atmosphere of the mine was neutral.

The radio crackled. "Dew? Dew? You there?"

It was Woody.

"Right here," Dew said, walking down the ramp, avoiding the goo that still glistened wetly.

"We're down in the Dry Room waiting for you. I think we better get while the getting's good."

"Ten-four on that," Dew told him. "On my way."

Had the mine just regained its sanity or was this the calm before the storm? He was confused, suspicious, but certainly not about to look the offered gift horse in the mouth. He went through the vestibule and under the archway and back into the corridor that led towards the front of the building. The Mess Hall and Dry Room were down there. Same old drab gray walls, scathed tile floors, the doorways, the bulletin boards. He got within fifteen feet of the Mess Hall when he stopped dead.

What the fuck?

There was a clock on the wall. He knew damn well it had to be getting on around midnight, but the clock said it was 8:14. He wasn't seeing this. He couldn't be seeing this. When they'd

58

originally come out of the Mess Hall, he'd looked at the clock and it had said 10:45. Maybe there was something wrong with it or maybe there was something wrong with everything.

He swallowed.

Panic surged hot and white inside him. Was this some kind of time distortion or a flashback or was he just fucking losing it? He stared at the clock. The seconds hand clicked slowly around. It was working. He could see that it was working. The panic was becoming terror now and he had the worst desire to scream.

And he knew why.

That neutrality he'd sensed just a few minutes ago, as if the malevolence had dissipated, was back in full force now. He could feel it gaining a sort of psychic volume around him like a guitar amp being cranked up.

8:15 now.

Don't you get it? Remember the texts on that phone. 8:15 is when it happened, whatever it was.

There was a sudden eruption of noise coming from the Mess Hall doorway. He nearly cried out at its intrusion. But it was nothing scary. In fact, it was perfectly prosaic: the sound of voices chatting, men laughing, cups being set down, forks scraping on plates. He could even hear a microwave oven humming and a radio playing a Brewers game in the background.

This is being offered to you, a voice told him. *A piece of the puzzle. Go in there and see what it's about.*

Yes, he knew that's what he had to do.

As he approached the doorway, there was the sound of running feet. Somebody was coming into the Mess Hall from the doorway at the other end. *"Hey!"* a voice called out, its owner sounding out of breath. *"They found something down in the pit! Something...something weird! It looks like a—"*

Silence.

It was as if a switch had been thrown. There were absolutely no sounds coming from in there now. Dew, tensing himself, went through the door and the Mess Room was exactly as it had been when he went in there with Jerry and Woody. Nothing was disturbed.

They found something down in the pit.

Is that where this nightmare started? Down in the pit? The idea of it chilled him and he was not really sure why. What could they possibly have found down there? Crazy ideas paraded through his mind and not one of them made any sense or could explain what was going on here.

The clock on the wall read 11:58.

Time had caught up with itself again. As he considered what that might mean, there was a sudden shrill buzzing. He swung around, his breath coming fast. The buzzing came again. It was the cell phone on the table. There was an incoming. He walked over there, trying to regulate his breathing. He picked it up and looked at the screen. It was the same as before:

8:16:32 Rip: gotta go something going on
8:16:39 Shell: what?
8:16:47 Shell: u there?
8:17:11 Shell: u alive over there?
8:18:36 Shell: Rip???
8:21:03 Shell: forget it

Except, he realized as terror filled his throat, there was something else now:

11:59:17 i am coming
11:59:31 i am getting closer

Dew badly wanted to throw the phone, but for some reason he did not. He was being played, he was most certainly being fucked with. But the knowledge of that did not stem the rising tide of fright in his chest. He stood there, his instinct telling him to run but his rational cop-sense telling him to stand his ground. His hand was shaking so badly he could barely hang onto the phone.

It buzzed again:

11:59:45 i can see you

It felt like Dew's heart was going to explode in his chest. His entire body was shuddering now. He reached down for his weapon and he could barely hang onto it.

11:59:57 i am right behind you

With a cry, he whirled around, bringing the gun up and he saw a slinking, worming sort of shape slip out the door and so fast he could not be sure what it was. Before he lost his nerve, he raced out into the corridor. It was empty. Perfectly empty. He waited there, fighting an awful, skin-crawling sort of sensation that he was being watched.

No more, no more. Deep inside, he was terrified by everything and yet the source of that terror was formless, completely without substance. He moved down the corridor at a hurried clip. He had his flashlight in one hand in case the lights went out again and his 9mm Beretta in the other. He cut back into the tunnel, his footsteps echoing around him, seeming unnaturally loud, and into one corridor after another and there, thank God, was the door to the Dry Room. He'd entertained a nagging paranoia all the way there that the corridors would go around and around in circles and he'd never reach his destination, only get that much more lost.

He went through the door.

He knew right away that Woody and Jerry were not in there. He had been baited, of course, and been so desperate to find his men that he took the offered candy and now here he was. The Dry Room was perfectly silent. At least, now it was. But something had happened here. It looked like a stampede had passed through, leaving destruction in its wake. The locker doors were all open, some were hanging by one hinge as if they'd been blasted open. Whatever had been in them—boots, jackets, lunch pails, magazines, newspapers—had been cast over the floor. Some of the lockers themselves had been yanked from the walls. A row down the center had been tipped over and tumbled about like caskets in a desecrated crypt. Safety posters and calendars had been ripped from the walls which were themselves cracked open in several places. One of the fluorescent light fixtures above dangled by a few wires, tubes flickering.

Looks like somebody that was extremely pissed-off, took out their rage on this place, Dew thought.

And it did.

Like some snotty-nosed, spoiled brat went on a tirade. There was no systematic destruction here, just wrath turned loose in every conceivable direction. But maybe it was more than that even, because he could smell the acrid, nose-reaming stench of urea.

Like an animal, they pissed all over everything when they were done.

What was he dealing with here? An intelligence, yes, but obviously one that was oddly childlike. It liked to play games, it liked to torment its victims like a precocious eight-year old monster pulling the wings off flies. It had temper tantrums, and apparently, it liked to piss on things like an animal marking its territory or a child fascinated by its own bodily functions as all children secretly were. He was long past thinking that what he was dealing with was human, much as the idea of a monster or an entity was completely against his own pragmatic belief system.

He walked amongst the debris, searching for something. He did not know what, but there was a concrete certainty within him that there was something, something he was brought here to see. And then...*yes,* there it was and at the sight of it, his heart began pumping hard in his chest again and his teeth locked together.

Written in black crayon on the white wall was the one thing he did not want to see, but perhaps knew he must see:

Yes, of course.

Just as it had been written on the wall of Dwight Rose's bedroom. *THEY MADE ME.* A childish scrawl in crayon, the work of a diseased mind collapsing into itself like a soft rotting pumpkin. It was not only what Dwight had written, but copied in the *way* he had written it. A perfect replica. So perfect that Dew might have been at the crime scene again. How many times after it happened had he dug the photos out of his locked filing cabinet and stared at them, particularly Dwight's parting words, trying to associate Dwight Rose the man with Dwight Rose the monster.

He had carried the trauma of it all within him for many years and whatever was haunting Superior Mine knew it. It knew just how to fuck with him, which memory hurt the worst and gave him the most dreadful nightmares. He thought perhaps he had buried it away, but it had always been there, rotten and black in the back of his mind, just waiting to be resurrected like a corpse rising from the mold of its grave.

Dew stood there, filled with conflicting emotions ranging from fear to hatred, self-pity to anger. *Dwight, fucking Dwight. We all knew you. We all trusted you. Then you went and destroyed those innocent girls. You made their deaths ugly and low. And what you did afterwards...you sonofabitch, you dirty murdering sonofabitch. I invited you into my house. I broke bread with you at my table. You drank my liquor. You pretended to be my friend and all the while you were laughing at us. A fucking monster. A ghoul. A pedophile. Swear to God if you were here right now, I'd fucking snap your neck, I'd—*

No, there was no point in working himself up. What would it solve? What had it ever solved? He had tortured himself with it for years and there was still no closure.

He had met Dwight through the bowling leagues. He seemed like a good guy and he came highly recommended. Everyone liked him. Looking back now, it seemed as if he had tried extra hard to ingratiate himself to Dew. Maybe something inside him was even then reaching out for intervention. Maybe he thought being close to a cop would keep his demons at bay. Regardless, Dew had invited him into his life, Dr. Jekyll and Mr. Hyde.

Dwight had helped him re-shingle the garage and put in the new bay window for the living room. Anytime you needed something, Dwight was there. This was how Dew ended up going fishing with him, inviting him over for cookouts and Sunday suppers. Freda, Dew's wife, was enamored of him. They had no children and Dwight, in a way, became something of a surrogate, a monster that hid behind a smiling face. Then those girls went missing. It hit Freda hard. The only one she knew was Brittany Richt whom was their papergirl and from whom they bought Girl Scout cookies for many years...still, it sent her into a tailspin that she never truly recovered from. She'd always had nerve problems, but with the missing girls it got worse. She couldn't sleep. She couldn't eat. She lost thirty pounds and began having dizzy spells. They prescribed Prozac to break her anxiety. It did little good. Then they put her on Paxil. Together, they shut her down almost completely to where she would do little else but sit in a chair and stare out the window. Then came the revelation of Dwight Rose and his secret life. Freda lost it. She started throwing away the silverware, plates, and glasses because Dwight might have used them. She scrubbed every surface in the house again and again and again that he might have touched as if what he had might be catchy. Her obsessive/compulsive behavior went on for some time and then Dew came home one night and found her in the tub, dead of what was later deemed an overdose. She swallowed nearly a month's supply of Prozac. But was it suicide or just confusion? As much as he wondered, he knew he would never really know.

That sound?

What's that sound?

Water running. He knew it wasn't the rain outside; he would never have heard it here in the Dry Room. Taking a deep breath, he navigated his way amongst the lockers going towards the back of the room. He stood before the doorway marked SHOWERS. Yes, this is where the miners went to cleanse the crud off them after a long day down in the pit.

Dew pushed the door open.

There was a tile wall with racks of freshly-laundered white towels and a couple industrial-sized hampers for the dirty ones.

A sign read: DON'T LEAVE TOWELS ON THE FLOOR. He moved past it to the shower room itself. Steam was coming out of there, billowing out like sea fog. The air was heavy, sodden, and warm, but Dew was shivering, his throat dry as cinders. The shower room was about thirty feet long, showerheads set in the walls at eye-level. They were all pushing out a fine, hot spray. There were no stalls, no privacy.

As he stood there, trying to gather up enough saliva to swallow, the showers turned off one after the other until there was only one still going. He could see a shape in the steam. Even from where he was, he could see there was something terribly wrong with it. Not a human shape really, but a gross exaggeration of one.

Maybe a wise man would have let it lay, but not Dew.

He stepped into the shower room, water sluicing past his boots to the central drain. It smelled like old sweat, grime, and institutional pine cleanser in there. His flesh tight as a drumhead on the bones below, he stepped closer to the figure until he was maybe fifteen feet from it. Slowly the steam dissipated and he saw what he knew he must see there: Dwight Rose. Still crusted with blood, he was a living atrocity. His face was more skull than face, the eyes huge hollow sockets, the crooked grinning mouth revealing teeth yellow and crumbling. His head sat on an angular stub of neck, his body covered in a brown-orange skin that was ropy and festering. The most obscene thing about it all is that in death, his proportions had become grotesque—the elbow of his right arm was down near his thigh, one shoulder raised in a pulsating mound, the other sucked down into a rugose cavity, the skeleton beneath it pushing through in a perfectly alien construction of bone.

I keep scrubbing and scrubbing and I just can't get the blood off myself, Dwight said, running hands like the scaly claws of vultures over the anatomical wreck of his body. *You shouldn't hate me, Dew. You should hate what was in me. I fought it for years and years until I had no strength left. I'd think of all those sweet little beavers on my softball team and that voice in my head, it would demand I do something. After awhile, it wasn't just whispering, it was screaming. All my life I'd been impotent with girls, but that changed the night I picked up Theresa Cestaro and took her for a ride. You remember Theresa, don't you, Dew? Long legs, those dark eyes and black hair. Yummy. Italian like a lot of them in this neck of the woods. When I told her what I had to do to her, she started crying, begging me not to hurt her...but that only turned me on. It was like foreplay. And when I got my belt around her throat and pulled it tight...oh Jesus, her eyes were bugging and she was gagging, squirming under me...it was too much. That's why I fucked her when she was dead. It was sweet release, Dew. I fucked her in the cootch and in the mouth and in the ass. I fucked her until she was all broken up and limp as a ragdoll. She was the first, my friend. And you always remember your first. I couldn't get enough of her. Even when she was green as Kermit's thumb, I was still screwing that hot little graveyard slut.*

Dew just stood there, horrified and disturbed and literally sick to his stomach because the Dwight-thing wasn't just explaining in detail what it had done, no, it was sending him images, letting him feel how it was to *be* Dwight Rose that terrible night. He could hear poor Theresa gagging, smell the sweat of her fear, feel her heart pounding under him as she died. Then he could feel what it was like to rape her corpse, the voices in Dwight's head shrieking with unholy passion the entire time.

It kept getting worse and worse until it reached a perverse crescendo and Dew had to escape the prison of Dwight's mind which was like a wriggling bucket of maggots he was sinking into. "SHUT UP! SHUT UP! SHUT THE FUCK UP!" he shouted and the psychic attack, if that's what it was, was broken off, and he felt the gun in his hand and by the time he realized it, he had jerked the trigger four times. Slugs ripped into the Dwight-thing and he cried out with orgasmic pleasure as they drilled through him.

Oh, if it was only that easy, Dew. See, I thought I was doing the right thing by killing myself. It was the only way out, the honorable way out, destroying the walking filth I had become. But it wasn't that easy. See, what was in my head, that thing that possessed me, it didn't want to die.

Dew stepped back, practically stumbling. There was an awful droning in his head that was sometimes Dwight's voice and other times, a sort of sentient buzzing. He had to block it out. Whatever it was, he had to block it out.

You can't block it out, Dew. What's in the pit won't let you block it out anymore than it would let me be dead. You can't fight it. It'll wear you down and own you and sooner or later, you'll do what it wants. Then your mind and your body will be like a vehicle that it drives and you'll...hah, hah...you'll just be a passenger. Because it has plans for you and Jerry and Woody just as it had plans for all those miners. We're all in this together, Dew, because nobody gets out alive...

Fucked with. Tormented. Tortured by his own memories and secret fears. That's what was going on here, Dew knew. Just as he knew he must fight against it. He had to overcome it or it would overcome him. He kept moving back and the form in the steam was just a shadow and he did not believe it really had much more substance than that.

"You're not real," he said out loud. "You're not really there."

Not real? Not real? You're wrong, Dew, you're so very fucking wrong! I'm the only thing that IS real! You are the one who is a dream and I can unthink you anytime I choose! I can make you unreal whenever I want, same way I can make it be right now or four hours ago or last fucking week! ANYTIME I CHOOSE, I CAN UNTHINK YOU! YOU GET IT? YOU GET IT, DIDDLY-DEW WITH THE COWSHIT ON HIS SHOE?

Dew tried to ignore the hissing voice in his head, but it was powerful. It was like trying to ignore the winds of a tornado as they blew your barn flat. He was confused, half out of his head, doubting what was real and what was not. He felt like he was drugged. Everything seemed slow, loose, and ungainly. His limbs felt heavy and his thought processes were alarmingly slow. He was still backing out of the shower room, one plodding step at a time. The steam before him was thickening into some white cobwebby mesh that seemed to glisten and sparkle as it was sucked into some ever-rotating vortex of mist.

He saw movement within its depths, a black and busy shape that was getting closer and closer. As he opened his mouth to cry out or shout, maybe both, he saw something come out of the steam. It looked like the spurred leg of an cricket, but enormous. He gauged that it was easily seven or eight feet long, a dull, dirty brown in color striated with yellow. It flexed on multiple joints, making a sort of chitinous clicking noise. There was no foot or pad at the end of it, only a slate-gray talon. It tapped across the floor like the cane of a blind man.

Another leg followed it and then another, all of them *tap-tap-tapping* away. They were connected to something massive and fleshy that was about to emerge from the steam, but Dew did not wait to see what it might be. Maybe it was real and maybe it was an illusion, either way it was deadly. If he thought it could hurt or kill him, then it damned well could.

He stumbled out into the Dry Room, tripping over a locker and then skidding on his ass on scattered debris. He had barely went down before he was up again, up and leapfrogging junk to reach the doorway and the corridor beyond.

Behind him, he heard a voice that sounded very much like his Uncle Jake, somehow given life on this dark and frightening night: *"GET BACK HERE, DEW! YOU HEAR ME? GET THE FUCK BACK HERE! YOU'RE ONLY MAKING THINGS WORSE ON YOURSELF!"*

But Dew, sprinting down the corridor, was willing to take that chance.

12

Woody thought: *You better watch him. He's ready to come apart. You better keep a very close eye on him.*

"You okay, Jer?" he asked.

"Fine. Now where's the door to that fucking garage?"

That was the question. It seemed like they'd been hunting for it for a long time now. Funny, when he thought about it, how it either seemed a very long time or not long at all. Time was either stretching out or it was compressed. And after what they'd seen on the clock in the office, he wasn't too surprised. Not that he was reading much into that. Bad clock, that was all. That's what he kept telling himself. It was easier that way. He didn't like to think that there was something else going on here, despite what he'd seen in the office. The idea that there was someone or, better yet, some*thing* behind this, left him cold. He couldn't have that. He needed to focus just as he'd been trained.

That's how Dew would do it. You know that. If you want to get through this, you have to think like him.

He moved down the corridor with Jerry tagging behind him like his kid brother in the funhouse at the fair. *And this sure is some kind of funhouse, all right.* More doors. Most of them locked. He stopped, feeling perplexed. In fact, *mystified* was maybe a better word for it. It seemed that the same corridors were repeating again and again. He'd seen Dew go down to the garage when they were in the office. It couldn't have been more than a minute in-between before Dew had walked out the door and appeared in the garage bay below. If that was the case, why the hell was it taking them so damn long?

"We're lost," Jerry said. "We're completely goddamned lost."

"We can't be."

"We are, Woody. I've seen this same corridor a dozen times now. When get to the end, we go left or right, it doesn't matter, and five minutes later we end up right back here."

Woody wanted to argue, but there was nothing inside him to argue with. Jerry was right. They were in a maze like the kind you saw on TV at English manor houses; it only made sense from above. Realizing this, he just stood there, feeling like a boy who'd wandered too far from his neighborhood and was hopelessly lost. It was a bad feeling. He was powerless, inept, incompetent…it deepened the sense of doom that gripped him with black claws.

"This is just great," Jerry said. "We know where Dew is, but we can't get to him."

"Just relax."

"You fucking relax. This is insane."

Woody sighed. "It's a big place, man."

"Yes, it's big, but it's not *that* big. Corridors always lead somewhere no matter how big a place is. They don't lead back to themselves."

"All right," Woody said. "You lead the way then."

Jerry usually had a cocky attitude concerning just about everything. So when he shook his head, refusing to take charge, Woody knew the man's confidence had all but dried up. He sympathized.

"I bet that if I run down to the end of the corridor and take a left or right, don't matter, I'm going to show up behind where we now stand," Jerry said.

No, no, that's bullshit, Woody thought. *Reality doesn't work like that. Physics are physics. They can't be reinvented.*

That was cool, rational thinking and it fell entirely flat in his mind. He didn't get it. He was handling things the way he figured Dew would…but it wasn't working, it just wasn't working.

He began to feel not just uneasy but downright scared.

"Jerry, let's just think here," he said, trying to sound calm even if he was lights years from it. "Let's be reasonable."

The lights went out.

Just like that.

Jerry let out a small, compressed cry. Woody thought he did, too. Within seconds, they had flashlights in their hands. Yes, the lights were out, but nothing else had changed.

"It wants to get us in the dark," Jerry said.

"What does?"

"Same thing that got those miners."

70

Woody didn't need this and mainly because he feared that it was true. "What do you suggest?"

"Well, Dew or no Dew, we have to get out of here. That's the first step. We've been in rooms with windows. Next one we find, we break it open and get out of here."

"And abandon Dew?"

"No, you knothead. We get outside and circle the building. That garage has to have a big-ass door. We find it and we go in that way."

Woody had to admit it was sensible. It was something constructive anyway. "Okay. Let's do it."

13

When Jay got outside, Tanya was leaning against the cruiser, her eyes wide and shining. She was shaking her head from side to side. Jay came right at her.

"ARE YOU OUT OF YOUR FUCKING MIND?" he shouted, little bits of white spit frothing on his lips. "YOU COULD HAVE KILLED ME! WHAT THE HELL WERE YOU DOING?"

And all Tanya could say was: "I don't know. I don't know anything."

He stomped around in a wide circle, stopping, then starting again, finally coming to rest, his hands on his hips. "There was nothing there, Tanya. You shot up a goddamned light fixture. That was all." He sighed, took off his hat and slapped it against his leg. "You're accountable for every one of those bullets and you know it. I wouldn't want to be you when Dale finds out. He'll eat you in two fucking bites."

He would have probably continued chewing on her—and he had the right since he was her superior in rank—but they both heard the radio from inside the cruiser. Jay jumped in and talked with whoever it was. Finally, he stuck his head out the driver's window. "Get in! We got injured people!"

Tanya slid into the passenger side and Jay was off, squealing through the parking lot, making for the road out.

"There's survivors down in the mine," he said. "They need help. They got dead and wounded down there. They're down in the Empire Pit. That's where we're going."

Tanya didn't like it. Her brain wasn't working so good anymore, but one thing she did know was that she did not want to go down there, down into the pit. *That's where it's all coming from,* she thought. *Doesn't he know that? Doesn't he feel that?* But he didn't. He was a cop and he was doing his job. She was the nutjob here, not him.

But dear God, down into the pit. Down into the awful pit.

She wanted badly to frame her dread and absolute horror of the pit for him, but there was no way he would understand and particularly after she had shot up the office. *Office? OFFICE? That weren't no office, ma'am, no sir my sweet apple dumpling,* a voice that sounded like an extra from an old western said in her head. *That were The Horror Chamber of Doctor Parasitius where the most godawful things can happen! But you're going to know alllllll about that, sugar plum, when your labia is licked to shreds!* She made an involuntary gasping sound because the voice wasn't her own mind toying with her. No...no, this voice was from beyond, from outside of her head. It was the voice of the thing down in the pit.

"Are you all right?" Jay asked her. "I mean, *really* all right?"

"Of course. I'm just fine," she managed.

"Then how do you explain what you did in the office?"

"How do *you* explain what you were doing as we drove in, Jay? You were about to have a psychotic episode."

"Don't exaggerate."

"I'm not exaggerating and you know it. Your eyes were bugging out of their sockets. You were fucking drooling."

She had him and he knew it. The very fact that he lapsed into silence was proof of that. Tanya very badly wanted him to admit something was seriously wrong at Superior Mining, but he kept his mouth shut. It was a very male sort of attitude: if you don't talk about bad things, maybe they'll go away.

"Here it is," he said, taking the turn to the Empire Pit.

Tanya felt like her skin was crawling. The paved drive was shining with pools of water, the dark woods pressing in from either side. She began to feel claustrophobic like she was being buried alive. Ahead, there were lights. A great many lights. Then the trees were gone and the road opened up and she saw piles of slag and crushed rocks higher than three-story houses. There was a maze of roads leading in every direction, all of them lit by sodium lights, signs directing the way to ore storage houses, primary crusher and grinding mills. It was like a city out here, buildings rising into the night. Everything was red with ore dust. Even the puddles were pink in the headlights. Dump trucks with massive fourteen-foot tires were parked in rows alongside immense saurian-like loaders and electric shovels. Everything seemed to be on a gargantuan scale.

"All this," Tanya said, "and not a single person around. Don't you find that just a little strange?"

They passed buildings that were three- and four-stories in height, all of them lit up. But she knew there were no people in them. They had all gone below. She didn't understand how she knew that, but she was certain of it.

Jay found the drive leading to the pit and Tanya's anxiety increased. The road followed a rise and from it, they could see the pit below like some gigantic meteor crater, its walls terraced with roads that slowly led down to the lowest level which was over a thousand feet below. It was well-lit by pole lights, but with the rain and mist, it looked murky and ominous like the world's largest open grave.

"Here we go," Jay said, clicking on the hi-beams as they began their journey down into the stygian depths. As they drove down and down and down, the road slowly winding around the outer edges of the pit, even the mist looked pink. The exposed rock was wet and dripping. The headlights of the SUV created vast, crawling shadows. The wipers swished back and forth, a pinkish residue on the windshield.

The radio crackled with static, then a voice came through. *"Is there anyone out there? Is there anyone that can help us? Dear God, we're dying down here...injured men everywhere...radio's not working! Why can't we call out? Even the cell phones don't work! Nothing works! Oh God help us! Help us!"*

Jay grabbed up the mic. "Sir! Sir! This is Trooper Nagle of the State Patrol. We are en route to your location. Please hang on. Help is on the way."

Tanya didn't like it. "Jay...this is a hoax."

"What are you talking about?"

"They're broadcasting on the police band. Doesn't that strike you as being a little suspicious?"

There was more crackling and the desperate voice went on as if it had not heard Jay at all. *"Alone...alone all the time...alone with the dead and dying and nobody cares. Nobody at all. I'll die down in this horrible godless pit in the darkness."* The voice was clearly sobbing now, wracked with pain. *"And where are the police when you need them? Where is help to be found when one is desperate and at the end of their rope? Where? I ask you. Goddamn where? Nowhere and never to be found. Eating donuts and chasing pussy, tasing old ladies and shooting down poor defenseless negros. A shame, a shame, a shame. Toy cops and little boy cops. Lots of gadgets and no common sense."* Now the timber of the voice had noticeably changed. It was no longer whimpering and afraid, but sardonic and calculating, speaking with a low hissing sort of tone, a Peter Lorry-esque intonation that people tended to use when they were imitating a child molester.

"Because if you truly had any fucking common sense, if you truly were out there to protect and serve, then you would stop the most horrible things from happening, wouldn't you? You wouldn't have let me do the terrible things I have done. And they are terrible, aren't they? One might say unspeakable, eh? Oh...remember...remember...all those dark, sweaty nights when I went into my step-daughter's room and looked down at her sleeping so peacefully, so pure, so innocent. That's why I had to defile her. That's why I put my grimy hands on her and shoved my fingers inside her and—"

"You shut up!" Jay said into the mic, his hand trembling. "You shut up with that fucking talk!"

Tanya just sat there in shocked, stunned silence as they moved farther and farther down into the pit and what waited there for them. Her breath hitched in her chest and her temples pounded, hot sweat breaking out on her face.

"...oh, but I loved it...I hurt her and I hurt her bad and that was the thrill," the voice went on, breathing fast now, clearly excited. *"The way she cried out, the tears in her eyes, the screams in the night as I pushed deep inside her, harder...harder...yes...YES, my darling! Yes...oh the sweet...the sweet...the sweet..."*

"FUCK YOU!" Jay shrieked.

"Jay," Tanya said, "we need to turn back! This is a trap! We're going into a goddamn trap!"

But he wasn't interested in that. He was sick to his stomach with what he was hearing and his professionalism was gone. The voice on the radio kept talking and he was getting more and more irate. He started hitting the radio with the mic, smashing it into it as hard as he could.

"Jay!" Tanya cried. "Jesus Christ, Jay! Get a hold of yourself!"

"Saying things like that," Jay muttered. "Awful, disgusting things like that. Goddamn animal. Goddamn monster."

The voice on the radio refused to die. Even when he turned off the system, they could still hear it cackling with delight. *"Fucking PIGS fucking COPS, you can't shut me off! Haven't you guessed why? Well, haven't you? Ha, ha, ha, roll them black-and-whites, you neo-Nazi SS knuckle-dragging Gestapo pricks! You're never, ever there when people need you. When they're dying slow, awful deaths down here, down in the darkness, down in the place I call home! Down here where I call the innocent, MY lambs, MY offerings, MY sacred sacrificial cows whose blood shall run in red rivers and wash MY feet and quench MY thirst! For that is their purpose, is it not? The human herd exists to satisfy ME, to fill ME, to enrich and empower ME! They are my wine and my meat and I cast their broken remains upon the waters like bread!"*

Jay was losing his mind, driving faster and faster down the road, deeper into the pit, deeper into the shadows of the netherworld, drawn in, baited, made ready like a suckling pig for the spit. Nothing Tanya said could stop him from getting down there.

He had to go.

He had to see.

He had to know.

And above all, he had to shut up that fucking taunting voice before his mind split right open and all the good things that made him Jay Nagle leaked out. He raced down the dirt road from one grade hewn from the rock to the next. They were almost there, almost there.

Tanya could feel the bottom of the pit getting closer, feel it reaching out for her like a hand in the darkness, eager to grasp her soft throat. She was filled with terror, beyond speech, beyond just about everything now. Knocked down to some infantile level where she could only gawk and whimper and tremble.

We're almost there, almost there. God help us, we're almost there.

And then Jay was moving the SUV down the final grade and she could see the bottom of the Empire Pit lit up with tiered construction lights. It was huge, looking about the size of a Wal-Mart parking lot. There were outbuildings and tool trailers and even a couple RVs. She saw rows of blue Port-O-Johns. Immense dump trucks and loaders, electric mining shovels with buckets that were so gigantic that they could have pulled the SUV in there and had room to do a U-turn. There were heaps of slag and gravel and raw ore. A sign read DANGER BLASTING AREA. It all looked perfectly ordinary. All it lacked was people. In the tall sodium lights, everything was illuminated a disconcerting yellow-orange. It was surreal and dreamlike.

The radio had been silent for a time. Even though Tanya knew it was all deadly serious and they were in unbelievable danger, she prayed it was all a joke. A sick joke, but a joke all the same. Then the radio crackled and a perfectly slick and reptilian sort of voice said, *"Ah, you've arrived. Your place has been made ready."*

After which, there was maybe twenty seconds of peace as Tanya's fear escalated, expanding inside her like a helium balloon. She knew, of course, that something was coming. That they were in the sights of a nameless thing malign and anti-human. She also knew that whatever it was, whatever had the ability to disrupt radio and cell communications and wipe out an entire shift at Superior Mining and maybe create spiders from Mars out of thin air, that this was its playground. And now that they were here, it would never let them go.

"I suppose we better take a look," Jay said.

He reached over to open his door and something rammed into the back of the SUV, making it bounce on its shocks. He let out a short, shrill scream that was half terror and half rage…then he threw open his door and jumped out. Tanya followed him, even though she knew it was pointless. The SUV, she saw, had been hit with enough force to crumple the back bumper and skid the tires four feet through the gravel.

She watched Jay go through his cop routine—legs spread, both hands on his weapon, arms extended. He aimed here, pivoted, then aimed over there, constantly in motion, performing his police kata like he was clearing a room of potential bad guys.

Tanya didn't even bother pulling her weapon.

What was the point? They wouldn't find anything to shoot at and what was hunting them would not show until it was time for the kill.

14

"This one will do," Woody said.

They were in an office and before them was a window. It was only a matter of shattering it and they'd be free of the goddamn building and the maze it contained. It was really very simple when you thought about it. And Woody had been thinking about it.

With Jerry at his side, he walked over to the window and looked outside. It was pitch black out there, maybe even darker than pitch. A seamless unbroken blackness like staring down into an open well by night.

"It looks funny out there," Jerry pointed out.

And it did. It really did. "We're in the back of the building," Woody said. "There's no lights back here. You'll see. We've got flashlights."

But Jerry did not seem convinced. "I've got a funny feeling about this."

So do I, brother, so do I. Woody thought this but there was no way in hell he was going to mention it. He popped the catch on the window, tried to slide it open but it wouldn't budge. Despite his reservations, Jerry got in there with him. They both put everything they had into it but it was no good. It simply wouldn't open.

"Whatever is haunting this place doesn't want us to leave," Jerry said.

Woody shook his head. "You're nuts."

"You know better."

And the thing was, he did know better. He felt it the same way Jerry felt it—that they were not alone, that something was in the dark with them, something was circling them just beyond their range of vision. Scanning about with his flashlight, he saw a metal airplane paperweight on the desk. He hefted it. It was solid. It easily weighed five pounds. He motioned Jerry out of the way and threw it at the window with everything he had. The paperweight bounced off it and clunked to the floor.

"It's not going to be that easy," Jerry said.

"All right, step way back," Woody said. He pulled his 9mm and punched two rounds through the glass. It shattered easily enough. There was nothing spooky about that and, hell, maybe he just didn't throw the paperweight hard enough. The only thing that really disturbed him was that as he went over to the window to pluck out the last few shards, the darkness out there seemed thicker than ever. Even his flashlight wasn't able to penetrate more than a few feet.

"See?" Jerry said, vindicated. "See? That ain't right. That ain't normal and you know it."

Woody didn't bother disagreeing. Things were fucked up in this place. The question being: was any of it real or was it all hallucination? The realist inside him told him that it couldn't be real, that if he tested the waters he would see how flimsy it all was like buildings on a Hollywood set that were nothing but facades with nothing behind them. Like those, he needed to kick this over and see if there was anything behind it.

Determined now, he said, "I'm going out. You wanna stay here and have a circle jerk with the spooks, you be my guest."

The amazing thing was, as soon as he announced this, it almost seemed like the darkness became that much darker until it looked like polished black glass out there. Not only that, but a horrendous, gagging, and positively revolting sulfurous stench blew in through the missing window as if there was an open sewer out there.

Jerry backed away. "No way. No way in fucking hell I'm going out there."

"Suit yourself," Woody said. "I'll circle around to the garage. Meet me there."

"You kidding? You want me to go out there again?"

"Either go out there or go out here."

Woody holstered his weapon and crawled through the missing window. His guts felt like they were filled with something thick and hot like bubbling molasses. But he couldn't back down; he knew that. This was now as much about proving there was nothing out there to fear as it was about saving face. He climbed out the rest of the way and dropped maybe five feet into the wet grass and melting snow. He started to climb to his feet.

"C'mon, Jerry. The water's fine."

Jerry said nothing.

Woody knew that he had to give him a minute. Jerry was tense, scared shitless. He would get his courage up, then slide through the window. He would have to. Not just to save face but because it was the only option.

"Jer, c'mon already."

There was a rustling inside the office. Something fell over. Jerry screamed. Woody got his head up to peek in there and that's when Jerry started shooting, busting rounds every which way.

Woody ducked his head down. "Jerry! For chrissake, quit shooting!"

There was nothing but silence from the office.

Woody put his head up over the sill, shining his light around. Christ. The desk was tipped over. The door was hanging by one hinge. There was wreckage everywhere, but there was no Jerry.

Woody swallowed, suddenly cold all over. "JERRY!" he called out. "JERRY! JERRY! WHERE THE HELL ARE YOU?"

There was no reply.

Woody thought he heard a rustling sound out in the hallway like a bed sheet on a line, but that was all. Something had happened in those precious seconds after he had hit the ground. Something terrible.

Jerry was gone.

15

The gunshots were what brought Dew deeper into the maze of the building even though he badly wanted to get out and return with serious reinforcements. They could have been a trick, of course, because the boogeyman of this particular nightmare knew very well how to play with his pets, how to torment his lab rats, the sort of cheese to offer them so he/she/it could draw them deeper into its trap.

But you don't have a choice and you know it, his mind informed him. *You're responsible for Woody and Jerry. Something happens to them, it'll be on your head...not to mention your conscience.*

Down the corridor he went, thinking the sounds had come from the general direction of the office overlooking the garage bay. That was somewhere he did not want to return to, but there was no choice now.

The tunnel...the intersecting corridors....it seemed like every time he came back it all got more snaking and confused. He tried his radio several times even though he knew it wouldn't work. Finally, he found the archway and went through it. There was the ramp leading up to the office. He noticed that the slime on the ramp was gone. Could it have evaporated? He doubted it. Maybe it was never there in the first place.

The door was shut.

Had he closed it before? He couldn't remember. That piss smell was gone as he tried the knob. The door was locked from the inside. Or was it? It was so hard to know what was real. He planned to get in there because something inside him told him it was important. But he wasn't sure if he could trust his instincts any longer. Maybe it was important and maybe he was just being toyed with, made to waste time and energy on a fruitless pursuit.

Which?

His heart rate increasing, his lungs pulling in deep breaths of air, his body readied itself for what it had to do. He threw his shoulder at the door and it gave, but it didn't come open. It was almost as if there was somebody pushing against the other side. He battered it three or four more times. It was like rubber, stretching open and then flexing back into shape.

Yes, he was almost certain someone was pushing from the other side.

He pushed against it.

Something pushed back.

He played the game once, twice, three times, then he pulled his Beretta and quite calmly put two rounds through the door. And maybe he wasn't thinking clearly, because a split-second after he'd squeezed the trigger he realized it could have been Woody or Jerry pushing back, broken by fear.

The door swung in.

There was no corpse sprawled on the floor. In fact, there was nothing. Nothing at all. The office was as he had left it. Then the shots hadn't come from here. All right. He would go room to room to room and he'd find where they came from or if it had all been a ploy. That was sensible enough.

He walked out the door and down the ramp, beneath the archway. Out in the corridor, he paused. That pervasive sweetness was in the air again. It was nauseating. Like inhaling the sweetness of honey that had brewed all summer in the heat.

Yet again, Dew had that crawling at his spine. The sense that whatever was running the show here was powering up for more fun and games. His throat went dry. His body felt oily with sweat as if he had been doused head to toe with warm cooking spray.

C'mon, you piece of shit. Do your damndest.

The lights flickered.

They went out.

Dew had his gun out by then. He clicked his flashlight on. In the shaking beam that made shadows curl and twist on the walls, he saw a dark form moving in his direction with the steady stiff-legged *clomp-clomp-clomping* of an automaton. He had drawn a bead on it. He wanted to shoot, but he was afraid to. What if it wasn't real? What if it was Jerry or Woody and his mind was made to believe it was something else?

It kept coming, *clomp-clomp.*

It walked like Frankenstein's monster did in old black-and-white flicks: an ungainly, rigid zombie-like shuffle. The stride of someone or some*thing* that had never walked before or, at least, in a very long time.

Dew swallowed. "Jerry? Woody? If it's one of you boys, call out now," he said as loudly and clearly as possible. "Something's playing tricks here and if I don't hear your voice, I'm going to start shooting."

The lights came back on.

The corridor was still dim and shadowy, but there was plenty of light to see by. He tucked his flashlight back into his belt and pulled his baton.

Okay, he thought. *Okay. No more games, time to heat things up face to face. Let's see how tough you are.*

The figure was about twenty feet away and now he could see it quite clearly. It was Dwight Rose, of course. It was him and it *wasn't* him. He was dressed in the same bloody clothes he'd had on that night they found his bled corpse in the shower stall. That much was consistent. But beyond that, it really wasn't him. No, this was Dwight Rose reimagined as a living human doll. His face and reaching hands were white as plaster, but shiny and plastic-looking. He had no eyes. There was black paint on his lips, a few tufts of hair sprouting from his skull. As he came on, Dew could plainly see that his synthetic face looked sutured as if it had been pieced together out of various rubber masks and that there was a fine purple-black vein networking just beneath the skin.

This thing was a monster.

It was not Dwight Rose, not really. It was merely a horror show representation of what people *thought* he was: the boogeyman incarnate, a lumbering Frankensteinian lunatic with all the soul of a scarecrow, a stalking shadow, an inhuman predator.

Dew wasted no more time.

When it was about fifteen feet from him, he pumped three slugs into it. It kept coming. Shooting this mannequin was like shooting a pine stump or a heap of graveyard earth: you couldn't kill that which was not technically alive. He put holes in it, but that was about it. No blood came from the wounds, only leggy skittering things that he knew were spiders. Just like the spider that had spun a web over Dwight's face in the shower stall. They were now part of him.

Dew's instinct told him to run.

That was the reasonable course of action, but he'd been running too long now. He put the Beretta away and waited in a defensive crouch, baton in hand. *This is crazy, this is suicide.* As Dwight reached for him, his guts felt like a cake of warm melting butter. He ducked out of its way, but it was faster than it looked. It clawed at his face with white fingers whose tips looked sharpened like No. 2 pencils. He barely avoided them. It pivoted quickly and slashed again. He sidestepped it and brought the baton down hard with an overhead swing, catching the creature square in the face which cracked right down the center, releasing more spiders that looked much like black widows—swollen, shiny blue-black bodies with needling legs.

Dirty fucking Pig! Rotten fucking baby-killer! he heard Dwight's voice shriek in the back of his head. *You went and made shit-work of my pretty shiny face!*

It giggled at its own joke and Dew swung his baton. But it saw it coming this time and managed to get away from the main force of his swing, taking a glancing blow to the side of its head which made Dew lose his balance momentarily. It seized the opportunity, jabbing out with a left fist that caught him in the ear. The impact was jarring. He staggered into the wall and just barely avoided the creature's clawing right hand. The fingers were like letter openers cutting four deep grooves in the gray wall.

It was driven into a rage now, screaming in his head, its claws cutting through the air like scythes. Dew found his feet before it went at him again and this time he didn't bother with any defensive moves, he went on the offensive. Jumping forward, he jabbed the business end of the baton into Dwight's face with enough force that a section cracked free and fell to the floor.

The creature brought its claws to bear, but he avoided them neatly and swung the baton, catching it in the arm. There was a distinct cracking and the lower arm swung from the elbow joint back and forth like a pendulum.

Dirty, dirty, dirty fighter! the voice cried, slashing out where Dew's head was a split second before.

He got behind it and when it came around he jabbed it in the face again, the remaining sections of its split face disengaging from one another noticeably. One side hung easily an inch below the other. It clawed. Missed. He jabbed it hard. The head sprung back on the neck as if it were going to fall off and then wobbled back into place, making a *thwaaaang* sort of noise like one of those flexible spring door stoppers do when you kick it. The head looked as if it had ratcheted up a few inches on the neck.

Like that game we played when we were kids, a voice in the back of Dew's mind mused in a hysterical voice. *The two fighting plastic robots in the ring. What was it called?*

Broken, cracked, bleeding spiders, Dwight came at him again with one working hand. Dew was going to finish it this time. By God, he was going to break this thing into pieces. When it got close, he side-stepped its slashing claws and, holding the baton in both hands, swung it like a bat. The impact was loud. The face split open in four directions. In Dew's mind, that hysterical voice said, *Rock 'em Sock 'em Robots, don't you remember?* And at that chosen moment, Dwight Rose's head suddenly popped up nearly a foot on its ratcheting neck, swinging from side to side. It no longer had a plastic doll's face, but a rubbery clownlike visage with eyes like melting chocolates. Hands came up and pulled its loose flabby cheeks out into flaps and its tongue looked like a bleeding braid of red licorice that wiggled in the air.

Dew felt something between a manic scream and deranged laughter crawl up the back of his throat. The world seemed to spin counter-clockwise on its axis. His thoughts were like dandelion fuzz blowing around in his head and he heard something like dozens of shrieking midnight cats mewing the music to "Twinkle, Twinkle, Little Star" and he knew he was struck mad, completely raving mad, crazier than a tapdancing frog, a fruit loop headcase who was nuttier than a jar of Planter's. And as sight, sound, and textual memory clashed in his head like cymbals, he remembered a Victorian print he had once seen of a lunatic making grotesque faces at himself in a mirror only it was *him,* it was Deuard fucking LaBay, the ding-a-ling general, the high sheriff of Crackershack, Wisconsin and resident wackadoodle headcase numero uno at the laughing academy.

Blah-blah-blah, blub-blub-blub, three men in a fucking tub, the Dwight voice cackled with wizened laughter in his head. *Bubble gum, bubble gum in a dish, how many pieces do you wish? Five ladies in a tub, one jumped out! And my mother and your mother were hanging clothes, my mother punched your mother right in the nose! Get it, Dew? GET it? C'mon, think! Do you know the muffin man, the muffin man, the muffin man? Well, you WILL! Hey...who hung his hat on the moon? Why, the owl in his bubble balloon! One bright summer night, he sailed out of sight and, hooting like Lucifer, hung in delight...can you dig it, Five-Oh? Can you book me on that, Danno? Can you?*

Dew heard himself scream in terror and madness. He felt everything inside him shrivel. He heard his voice sobbing only it wasn't him *now* but him *then:* eight-year old Diddly-Dew with the cowshit on his shoe. Everything was whirling around him and his brain was going to mush and his willpower was tapioca pudding. His guts were stuffed with globs of white bread soaked in water and some vile, formless substance that his dreaming infantile brain told him was snail putty and boogersnot. He was caught between this world and the next, only the pull of the next was much, much stronger.

This was beyond madness, beyond ordinary lunacy, this was a feverish and hallucinogenic glimpse of some surreal anti-world that had no true physical laws. Toys were people that were zombies that were monsters that were toys. The sky was blue taffy and the clouds were cotton candy. Tulips in the garden giggled while orchids wept and roses screamed. Windows bled if you scratched them and houses were made of juicy red meat that huge rats fed upon as they avoided cats that walked upright like men and frogs with the teeth of sharks. And through all the topsy-turvy, inside-out and upside-down madness, men and women writhed across the ground in boneless S-shapes like grass snakes, and—

Bang!

He thought his head exploded but it wasn't that at all. Old bleeding clown-face Dwight Rose had tucked him away in a cocoon of cosmic dread and once he was weak and whimpering, it had punched him right in the face. *Punched?* Hell no, it had pile-drived him right to the canvas. He hit the floor, stars exploding in his head. He had dropped the baton and his upper lip was split neatly open. Blood was in his mouth and on his teeth and dripping down his chin.

And that's how we play THAT game, Dew!

Dwight reached for him there on the floor and just as its claw-hand would make contact, Dew moved. The pain woke him up and made him angry because he was no quitter. He was a guy who never gave up. That's what he always told himself. So he braced himself against the floor and kicked out, catching Dwight in the knee with the flat of his boot and *crack!* the knee was dislocated and Dwight fell against the wall. And before it could recover itself, Dew was up with the baton in his hand bringing it down on the creature's head until it completely shattered. Headless it tried to get up, but it couldn't get its knee under it and it fell over, trembling and going still.

Ohhhh...you got me, Dew! You got me!

And then as Dew watched, leaning breathless against the opposite wall, the remains began to inflate. They swelled into an oval sphere, Dwight's clothes ripping free from the expansion. And Dew thought: *An egg, that's an egg, a sphere...a cell. Yes, a cell. It's one cell but if you don't get a handle on it, it's going to start dividing and there'll be two and then four and then eight and then sixteen and thirty-two and sixty-four...and how many will it take until the human race are playthings and livestock and then are no more?* He drew his weapon and fired into the egg cell until his 9mm was empty.

But it was hopeless.

Entirely hopeless.

All he did was help it split open and then he saw something in there, something dark and shifting and fluid. Then it cracked wider and slime that was gray-green spurted out and he saw what he had seen in the shower room: a long jointed leg that was spurred and striated and blotched purple. It came out and tapped on the floor and then there was another and another as the thing was born again, maybe the way it had been born down in the mine. The legs dripped with some stringy yolky material and he figured if he waited long enough, the legs would keep coming until they filled the corridor.

Dew backed away, seized with horror and dread at his insignificance and the omnipotence of his enemy that in the back of his mind was something from beyond time and space that could fill the known universe with its expanding form.

And as he stumbled down the corridor, the voice of the thing in the egg said, *"Hang around, Dew…hang around. I'm just getting going. I haven't really been born yet. Wait until I'm all the way out. It's like nothing you can imagine. Wait until you see the real me…and you do want that, don't you, Dew?"*

But shaking from head to toe, Dew knew he didn't want that at all.

16

Alone now.

Jerry was alone in the dark and he had lost his flashlight. *Lost it, dumbass? It was taken from you! Taken by the thing that haunts this place.* Woody had slipped out into the night and then some horrid monstrosity came out of the dark. In his flashlight beam, he saw…God, he wasn't even sure now…eyes and teeth and claws. He started shooting. Then he ran, ducking behind the first door he found in the darkness.

Now he waited.

He had given up on Dew and Woody was probably toast, too, which meant he was alone and he'd have to think himself out of this. He didn't like that. He always counted on Woody and Dew for things like that. He was no coward. Point him the right way and he could be very aggressive…but he still needed pointing.

Just think now, he told himself. *All night this…this phenomena has been following a pattern: bursts of activity followed by a lull. You might be in a lull right now. If that's the case, now is the time to move.*

That was good thinking, but the idea of having to navigate himself by feel alone, well, he didn't like it much. Too bad. It had to be done. He wasn't going to die here. After all, he had things to live for.

He raised himself up.

He still had his 9mm and his baton. He knew how to use both. If he could master his fear, he could get out of here and back to his life, back to Marianna. God, how he wished he were with her now. But there was only one way to accomplish that.

Okay.

He knew where the door was; that was a start. He crept over there. This would be easy, if only he could keep his head. He became aware of a sudden chill in the air that seemed to be escalating by the second, filling the room with frost. There was a smell, too, a sharp and nasty odor. It reminded him of embalming fluid, things pickled in jars. Then another odor insinuated itself: a dark sweetness that was heady and repulsive, the stench of things rotting in black cellar holds.

He knew by then that he was no longer alone.

"Who's there?" he asked, keeping his voice firm and steady.

"It's only me, Jerry, it's only me, my sweet, my precious," a woman's voice said and for one frightening/exhilarating moment he thought it was Marianna. But no, this voice was older. It was smooth and velvety. *"And you can trust me."*

He didn't believe that for a moment. He still had his Nokia in his pocket. He'd forgotten about that. It would be easy to light the room if he wanted to. The white screen would do the trick.

"Who are you?" he asked as he slid his baton into his belt, trying to make no sound.

"I'm a friend. I may be the only friend you have. That's why I want you to think very carefully about what it is you're doing, okay?" The voice was very nice and it relaxed him. *"Out there in that corridor there's death. It's waiting out there with claws and teeth to spring on you. Your gun won't do you any good because it's too fast. It'll tear out your throat before you can say, well, Deuard LeBay."*

Jerry wasn't exactly naïve. He knew there was trouble brewing here. His instincts told him to put a couple rounds in the direction of the voice and run like hell. But at the same time, his common sense told him to wait, see what this person had to say.

"That's good thinking, Jer."

"How the hell do you know what I'm thinking?"

There. He had the baton in his belt and now he began to inch his hand up towards the pocket where he kept his phone. He did it very, very slowly.

The voice sighed. *"I know lots of things. You'd be amazed at what I know and what I can find out. Right now, for instance, I know that you're alone. That Dew is dead and Woody is laying out there in the rain with a twisted leg. Try me, I know all kinds of things."*

His hand was at the pocket now. It was only a matter of carefully unsnapping it. "Who the hell are you?"

The voice tittered. *"It doesn't matter WHO I am, Jer. That's the least interesting thing of all. The important thing is that I can help you. I can get you out of this mess if you'll just listen to me, trust me."*

"I don't have time for your games," Jerry told it, his face beaded with sour, fear-smelling sweat as his hand unsnapped the pocket flap. "If Woody's hurt, then I need to get to him."

"You sure you want that? Are you really sure?"

"Yes."

He was sliding the phone out now.

"I think that would be a very stupid idea just like using that phone to light up the room. A real stupid idea. You better put it away while you still can...because soon as you light up this room, those things out in the corridor are going to leap through the door and tear your guts out."

Breathing hard, the fine hairs at the nape of his neck standing up, Jerry brought up the phone. And as he did so, from the doorway not three feet away he heard rustling. The padding of large hairy feet. A low growling. A violent, gamey animal stink flooded into the room. It was hot and foul. The stench of something that lived in a cave littered with the bones and hides of its prey.

"You better watch it, Jer."

He stepped back away from the doorway. He didn't know what to do. He was afraid of what was out in the corridor. Maybe it was nothing, maybe it was just another mind fuck being played on him...but did he really want to take the chance? No, of course not, but being in here, in the dark, with what was speaking to him, that wasn't good either. Inside, he was panicking.

"The question here is: do you really want to go help Woody?" the voice asked him. *"A guy you can't really trust. A guy who is lusting after your girlfriend. A guy who's already hit on her and has every intention of getting her into bed—"*

"Shut up! You better shut up or I swear to God I'm going to shoot!"

"Easy, Jerry, easy. I hate to be the one to tell you this...but you know you've been suspecting it. That's the problem with beautiful women. They're like collector's items and every idiot with a dick wants to own one. You've got one and Woody wants

her. It's only a matter of time before he seduces her. You know that, don't you?"

Suddenly, Jerry wasn't afraid.

Not really.

Yes, he'd been jealous as hell ever since he'd been with Marianna and maybe this is why. It was one thing for idiots on the street to stare at her, but Woody...Woody was his partner. Woody was his friend. That sonofabitch. Smiling to his face and stabbing him in the back. What a fucking guy.

"I should kill him," Jerry said out loud without even realizing it. "That's what I should do."

The voice laughed. *"Don't do anything hasty. He'll get his. You can trust me on that."*

But Jerry didn't trust the voice.

He trusted nothing about it.

There was something blatantly evil about it, something cunning and manipulative. He knew he could no longer trust Woody, but he didn't really believe he could trust this voice either. He swallowed. The phone was in his hand.

"I'm your friend, Jerry. You need to believe that before it's too late."

"Like hell you are," he said.

He clicked on the white screen and saw a shape crouched in the corner, a dark hunched-over sort of shape like a scarecrow without a bracket to hold it up or a marionette with clipped strings. It had a head that looked like an old gunny sack, a ragged hole cut for the mouth and two others for the eyes. There was nothing but blackness in them.

The sight of such a thing in the uneven, jumping light of the Nokia made a scream come rushing out of him before he could stop it. He fired twice at the shape, one of the rounds going straight through its head and leaving a smoldering hole where its forehead should have been.

The shape climbed to its feet and Jerry fired at it and kept firing until his gun was empty. The shape was oblivious to bullets. It came on with a lumbering tread as Jerry tried frantically to find the door. He felt around, hands fumbling, phone dropped. A wet stain steamed at his crotch. Sack-head moved in his direction.

"If friends don't have trust," its voice said. *"They have nothing."*

It pulled the sack free with wormy, flaking hands and Jerry looked at something that was beyond anything he had ever seen before. He could literally hear his mind shear open, his sanity venting itself in a single hysterical cry. He turned to flee and smashed right into the doorframe. The impact dropped him and he saw the horror standing over him, its face crawling like maggots in the light of the dropped Nokia.

"Open your mouth, Jer," sack-head told him. *"If you don't, I'll rip it open and I'll take your face with it."* Sack-head's left hand was not a hand but long yellow curving claws.

Jerry erupted inside, stumbling to find his feet, reaching out for the darkness of the corridor. He almost had it, but sack-head grabbed him from behind and smashed his face again and again into the doorframe. He went limp in its grip. He was barely conscious as it spun him around and those claws peeled his lips free, digging into his mouth and snipping his tongue like a ribbon.

Jerry came to, his mouth full of blood. It bubbled from his lips and gurgled in his throat as he spat out the meaty flap of his severed tongue. The pain was debilitating. It sucked the wind from his lungs and the thoughts from his mind. The room spun and he went out cold.

The throbbing agony brought him back out of it within seconds and he could hear himself sobbing, his face wet with blood and tears.

Sack head still stood over him. *"Open your mouth, Jer,"* it said. *"Open it now or I'll take your balls."*

Whimpering, out of his mind, thrashing on the floor, Jerry parted his lips and that made the pain flare white-hot in his mouth. Sack head pulled something out of his pants, only Jerry did not want to see it. It wasn't until the hot yellow stream was directed at his face with considerable pressure did he realize he was being pissed on. The urine bit into his skin like acid, searing his eyes shut and swelling his eyelids purple. It burned his face and filled his mouth like boiling water. The stench was sharp and bitter like drainage from a battery with a curious unclean after-odor of urea, gallons of it.

Somewhere during the process, Jerry's mind just shut down and he was grateful for it.

17

"Jay, please," Tanya said. "We need to get out of here."

"No. I'm going to find who's doing this."

He moved off ahead of her, walking faster and faster and she knew she should keep up but the faster he went, the slower something inside her seemed to run. She was tapped out. She barely had the strength to stay on her feet. Each plodding step took immense amounts of strength and endurance. The muscles of her legs were aching as if she had just walked five miles or run a marathon. Even her arms felt flaccid. She felt like she hadn't slept in days.

"Jay…please…"

But he was already far ahead of her in the rain.

He cut between two huge piles of gravel and by the time Tanya got there, he was navigating a heap of schist and loose rubble, scrambling to the top and disappearing from sight. She tried to climb up after him, but everything shifted beneath her and she kept falling down. Her uniform was pink with clay and ore mud. She tried two more times and when she fell down yet again, she did not move. She simply laid there, her eyelids heavy, her body feeling like cement, rainwater running down her face and soaking her to the skin.

Then a voice stirred her.

A wild, shrieking voice.

Jay? Jay? What?

She pulled herself up, balancing on her hands and knees. She felt a little better now that she wasn't trying to catch up to him and his long athletic strides.

"TANYA!" she heard him call. *"TANYA!"*

The sound of his shouting brought her up and out of her lethargy. She got to her feet and began the climb to the top of the rubble and when she got there, she could see him on a rise in the distance. He was swinging his flashlight back and forth like a beacon. She signaled him back.

And as she did so, she thought: *Why? Why are you doing this and why is he doing this and what do either of you hope to accomplish by killing yourselves?*

Those were the questions of sane, rational minds but she did not honestly believe that either Jay or she were necessarily sane anymore. She didn't think they were ready for the bughouse, but they were close, real damn close. They were acting irresponsibly...particularly for cops. The voice on the radio had pulled Jay down here and, God help her, she went along for the ride. That was what this was about. Simple police work—someone needed help, you crawled through shit to see that they got it.

Except there was more to it than that.

Ever since they'd gotten down here, there had been more going on. Things had been happening under the skin. She'd felt it: a sort of magnetism. Despite the fact that she was terrified and her belly was flip-flopping with adrenaline-laced apprehension...she *wanted* to come down here. Something in her wanted to see what it was all about and would be satisfied with nothing less. There was a skin-crawling, spine-tingling exhilaration to it all.

She was down here at the bottom of the Empire Pit because she couldn't conceive of being anywhere else.

The pull was that strong.

"GET OVER HERE!" Jay shouted, slapping her back into reality. "YOU GOTTA SEE THIS!"

She scrambled down the other side of the heap, sliding on loose scree and tearing her pants and getting gravel up her shirt. Her hands were filthy as was her uniform. But she didn't care. She really didn't care. She had to see what Jay found. She found her feet and raced to the slope he stood atop. *I'm coming,* she thought. *Oh Jesus, yes, I'm coming, I'm coming!* And even as the words spooled through her brain she knew that they didn't sound right. It was like something you might call out at the hot apex of an orgasm...and she wondered if that wasn't closer to the truth than anything else.

The slope.

Here it was, here it was.

She scrambled up it, cutting her hands on sharp plates of rock and not even caring. When she was nearly there, Jay reached down and hoisted her to her feet and she had the worst and most inexplicable desire to wrap herself around him. Worse, had he asked her to take him in her mouth nothing could have stopped her from dropping to her knees.

Christ, girl, what's wrong with you? What's in your head?

But she didn't know and she didn't care; she only hoped that she'd never have to live without it again.

"What is it, Jay?" she heard her voice say. It was breathless, practically panting. The words felt hot in her mouth. She wiped drool from her lips, leaving a dirty streak on her face like war paint.

"Down there," he said. "Down there…"

In the dull orange sodium lights she could see a shadowy dark hollow in the floor of the pit that had to have been fifty feet across. From her position, it looked very much like a moon crater, except that it wasn't so perfectly round. Jagged, actually, like a yawning mouth filled with broken teeth. The hollow…no, no, *crater,* because that's what it was…looked deep and it should have been dark, but it wasn't. The walls were flickering with a curious green fire like auroras. It made shadows jump around the edges like dancing figures.

Tanya shook her head side to side, her breath rasping in her throat. Her muscles were bunched. Her tendons and ligaments strained, the hairs on her arms standing on end.

Jay made a squealing sort of sound and raced down the face of the slope and Tanya went after him. Both of them were slipping and sliding, fumbling and tumbling like two kids rolling down a sand dune in pursuit of a beach ball.

Finally, holding onto one other, gasping and rigid, they stared down into the crater and Tanya made a cooing sound in her throat she was not even aware of because…well, because it was like the crater was a huge green eye staring up at them.

"There's a ladder," Jay said.

Yes, of course there would be a ladder. If there wasn't, how would you get down there? Because you *had* to get down there. What other choice was there? Then she noticed something that she hadn't noticed before in her excitement—the crane, the massive crane that was pitched over on its side, perched on the far edge of the crater. It looked like it might go rolling down at any moment. It looked, in the shadowy light, like some dinosaur laying dead in the gently falling rain. Rather like one of those illustrations you saw in old books about the extinction of the dinosaurs—huge beasts lying about rotting. And as she looked at it, a light seemed to go on in some dark attic room at the back of her brain. *They used dynamite. Yes, they used dynamite to clear an outcropping. Then the crane...a mining shovel...had gone in to clear the rubble and it had broke through the thin rocky veil over the crater.* She thought about that. About the crater. Way, way down here, a thousand or so feet beneath the surface encased by solid rock. How long would something like that take? How many eons? How many untold millions and millions of years?

Then that light in the attic room got brighter.

She thought...no, she *knew* that once the shovel had broken through and the crater was exposed for the first time in hundreds of millions of years, that the crane operator was seized by what was seizing her. He crawled out of the cab and climbed down off the crane and into the crater where he leaped and shouted and pretty soon, everyone down in the Empire Pit had come to see what he had found.

But that wasn't all.

No sir.

Within twenty minutes, everyone up in the main offices was on their way down, too, forming a parade line in the rain because they were drawn to it. They had to see. In fact, some of the workers from above were so overwhelmed that they climbed the security fence around the Empire Pit and dove to their deaths far, far below. And if Tanya was to look, she would find their smashed remains lying about, huge moonstruck grins on their dead faces.

Jay was moving down the ladder now, mumbling under his breath.

Tanya stood above, dirty and dripping, shaking with conflicting emotions and physical desires. She felt hungry. She felt horny. She felt confused and dizzy and energized. It was like something inside her wanted to burst right through her skin. The mud on her face and hands felt warm. There was thunder and lightning inside her, boomers rolling through her head. Her eyes were huge and unblinking, shining in their sockets like wet chrome. Her nipples were hard as pegs and in-between her legs there was a molten zone like hot butter. A combination of heart-pounding ecstasy and sweet terror rushed through her like hissing steam and she had the strongest need to masturbate, to slide her fingers into herself as she squirmed in the mud and puddles, eyes rolled back in her head, mouth agape, and brain burning with a delicious carnal fever.

Oh, the magnetism of what was down there.

The power and purity and rapture of the thing.

She couldn't wait any longer. She sped down the wet rungs of the ladder like a monkey down a vine and stumbled over to stand near Jay. The forks of emerald fire were still licking up the walls of the crater and their source was an oval depression right at its center. Tanya stared down in it. It was probably fifteen feet in width and whatever had been in there—oblong sphere, egg, whatever—it had hatched now. Whatever had gestated in the oval for so very, very long, had been born now, had been awoken from its dormancy when its birth chamber was disturbed. There was a sort of flaccid rubbery membrane down there that had been sheared open. The dying green light made it look glossy and veined.

What was it? she wondered, needing to know the nature of it. Nothing had ever been so important to her. Then, it came to her and she knew, she *knew.*

A cell, her mind told her. *A cell. A single cell of something much larger. A cell in the biological definition in that it was the most basic functional unit of a particular type of life form and also a germ cell, an origin cell...and also a cell as in a containment area, a cage, a prison. What was in there wasn't meant to get out, but now it has. And what do you think of that?*

She didn't like it, yet she couldn't help but be drawn to that oval, which in its own way was the nucleus of the crater much like a nucleus of a cell. There were voices screaming in her head that she refused to listen to, voices that were warning her away from this place and telling her in no uncertain terms that she was in incredible danger.

You're not thinking, you're just not thinking, they told her. *You're acting like a fucking drone, a robot, a walking piece of meat with instinct...but not a rational human being. Your buttons have been pressed, your neurotransmitters have been hijacked...you, my dear, have been played...*

And then it all peeled away, the sexual tension, the hungry anticipation, the manic craving. It was gone in an instant. What had been trying so very, very hard to reach her, to make a connection, to get through the psychological fog succeeded and all those bright, burning, beautiful lights went out...and there she was, Trooper Tanya Seatin, caked with filth from head to toe, standing there with her mouth hanging open as an unbelievable horror filled her, her blood draining away, leaving her weak and woozy.

She went down to her knees, dry heaves making her convulse on the muddy floor of the crater.

And just as she did so, Jay said, "I see it, Tanya, I really...fucking...see it..." He was reaching out his hands into dead space as if he were trying to grasp something, contain it, understand its form and shape. "What was in the...the...the cell...what it...*oh Jesus Christ, oh Jesus fucking Christ—*"

He stumbled away with widening eyes, his mouth opening and closing, emitting a series of panicked shrieks. His hands went to the sides of his head. He stumbled, he shook, he tripped over his own feet and went down. And then, like some frightened animal, he scurried up the ladder before Tanya could even hope to stop him and she heard him screaming into the night.

She was alone.

Alone in the crater.

18

It was all pointless, Dew realized. You couldn't fight against something with the immensity of what came out of the pit. It could manipulate your every thought, your every action. It could twist reality and warp time and bring ghosts out of the grave of your subconscious. What he needed to do was to come back with reinforcements. That was the thing. That was logical. That was practical. That was bare bones common sense. Come back in with thirty cops that were ready to bust heads and bag the bad guys.

Or get bagged.

And if that didn't work, blast this fucking place flat.

Still...the voice of his conscience tormented him, repeating the same thing again and again in his head: *It's one cell but if you don't get a handle on it, it's going to start dividing and there'll be two and then four and then eight and then sixteen and thirty-two—*

Bullshit.

He walked right out the front door, the way he had entered with Woody and Jerry and nothing tried to stop him. Which meant, either the entity from the pit was taking a siesta and recharging its psychic batteries or it didn't really give a shit what he did.

Out the door and into the parking lot and there he stopped.

The lights flickered and went out and he thought, *not this again, not the same bullshit, plunging me into the dark,* but then they came on again and he saw that every vehicle was flipped over and smashed. They looked like they'd been put through a car crusher and then dropped from a hundred feet above. The parking lot was an automotive graveyard of mangled metal. There was shattered glass, twisted steel, ruptured tires, and broken plastic everywhere. All of it sitting in a lake of oil and transmission fluid that glistened in the lights like spilled blood.

The only vehicle untouched was his SUV.

It was sitting there, waiting for him. He wondered briefly if he was fool enough to get into it because if the entity could get into people's heads, if it could warp reality and create monsters, then surely it could invade and infect an ordinary internal combustion engine. He thought of horror movies where people always did the wrong thing at the wrong time, poked their noses in where they didn't belong and wandered off to places that put them in mortal danger.

Was he that much of a fool?

He knew he was because all he could think of were his deputies and their families and if he did not have help, they stood no chance. Maybe they were already dead. If not, they certainly would be if he didn't marshal some forces. If he tried to make it down to Mineral City on foot, it would take a good thirty minutes if not an hour and he just didn't have the time to waste.

Do it then. Because there probably isn't a Mineral City anymore.

He hopped behind the wheel and turned the SUV over. It started, of course, as he knew it would. He tried the radio, but it was still an ocean of static. Same as before. And like before he could hear that breathing noise just underneath it. Terror filled his throat at the sound of it because he knew there was something out there, something listening. It was not imagination. The thing from the pit was there and he could hear it…maybe just in his mind, but it was there, all right.

Carefully, though his hands were shaking, he reloaded his Beretta and made ready because he was many light years from being safe and he knew it.

Swallowing, he put the SUV in drive and cruised through the lot, waiting for the boogeyman to show. But he, she, or it did not. Dew drove through the lot and out onto the incoming road without interference. Then, as some struggling flame of optimism began to burn brightly inside him again, the cab was filled with that same ultra-sweet stink he had smelled before and everything crashed inside him. It kept getting stronger until he became woozy with it and he had to pull over. He opened the windows but it did no good—it grew more pervasive until it wasn't a cloying sugary smell but one of sweet putrescence.

He was afraid.

He realized then he had never not been afraid, though this was definitely worse, like some hot seam of pure terror was burning in his chest. He was worried that the world around him would begin to dissolve into madness as it had when he faced off against the Dwight Rose thing. He couldn't allow it. He had to keep his head.

"That's right," a voice next to him said. *"It's never been more important than it is right now."*

Dew nearly screamed—Dwight Rose was sitting next to him.

He was an absolute horror, a rotten, putrefied thing that had crawled from a grave, an animate zombie puppet. His face was green and spongy, his lips like torn gray vinyl, his eye sockets filled with flies. When he smiled—and he did smile—his teeth were black pegs sunk in cancerous brown-purple gums.

"Drive, Dew. Put this thing in gear and take us below to our appointed place because that's where it's going to happen, that's where you and I are going to square off," Dwight said, a mucid sound to his voice as if the lining of his throat was peeling off in curds. *"None of these others are giving me much entertainment. They're not up to the job, but you are, Dew. I know it. You've got guts and gumption and iron in your pants. You are one stubborn prick and I can't wait until we butt heads. It's fated, ain't it?"*

The insane thing was that Dew *was* driving.

By the time he pulled his head out of the clouds (or out of his ass, take your pick), he was driving down the road, wheel in hands. Taking a leisurely Sunday drive with a breathing human carcass that looked like it had crawled out of a Bernie Wrightson comic. The rain fell and the wipers swooshed. Shadows, oddly fat and phantasmagoric, danced about like wraiths. And far above, peering through the leaden gray haze there was the moon. He knew if he looked at it, it would wink, so he looked everywhere else.

"I know you got ideas in your little pea brain, Dew, but just forget 'em. Your gun can't hurt me but I can hurt you in ways you can't imagine. For instance, right now as we speak, I got Woody and Jerry down in the pit with the rest of the miners." The oozing voice let that lay. *"If you piss me off, I'm going to*

break their minds with their own memories, turn their brains into warm gray paste, then I'll pluck off their limbs like the wings of flies, one at a time...and you know what, Dew? You know what, Diddly-Dew with the cowshit on your shoe? I'm gonna make you hear them die. I'm going to play it full volume in your head and you'll never be able to turn it off, never, ever, fucking ever."

It knew his every move.

Even as it warned him against pulling his gun, the Beretta 9mm was already in his hand. Dwight sighed as if he was disappointed and there was a smacking sound like sticky lips opening and his face distorted, a black slime running out of his mouth and eyes. Though Dew had not touched the buttons, the windows slid shut.

"I can fill the cab with...ME...and you can drown in...ME," the Dwight thing said.

Dew, making a sort of moaning sound in his throat, felt his hand slide the Beretta back into its holster. He felt his strength ebb. His willpower, resolve, everything went with it. He was like a leaking balloon. Everything inside him drained away, all of it gathering in his chest and following the lines of gravity down into his boots. He was loose and boneless. There was a resounding crack inside his head that was the sound of his mind splitting open. The SUV, with no hands on the wheel and no foot on the accelerator, rolled to the side of the road and bumped into a melting wall of snow pushed there by a plow. There was a high screeching sound in his ears and then a stench of dampness, of rot, of decaying vegetables in a root cellar, gassy and horrific. And he knew this was the true smell of the creature sitting next to him. The thing from the pit. The enemy.

It started speaking again, its breath foul beyond belief like the stink of wads of cotton stuffed in the belly of a dead man to absorb drainage: *"I called them down into the pit, Dew. I made them all come to sit at my feet and worship me. And they couldn't wait. They rushed down below because they could not refuse me. Some of them were in such a hurry they leaped...but you'll find out all about that when you get down there, when you are in my court and I grant you an audience with the king..."*

And then it was gone.

Dew was alone in the cab.

His strength gradually returned and he grabbed the wheel, jamming down on the gas pedal, the SUV vaulting back onto the road, fish-tailing in the mud and slush. After a minute or two, he slowed and only because he was at the fork in the road. If he went straight, he was out. If hung a right, it would take him where Dwight wanted him to go: down into the bowels of the Empire Pit where a horror beyond reason waited.

He pulled to a stop.

What if Jerry and Woody were really down there?

And what if it *really* was a cell making ready to divide? Did he have the right to run if running meant that he cursed the entire human race to doom? He didn't know. He was confused. His instinct told him to get the hell out of there, but his ethics, his morality, his cop's sense of law and order told him that he had to go down there because it was not only his job as a police officer but as a man.

Swallowing down an ocean of darkness that filled him to the brim, he hung a quick right before he could talk himself out of it. That thing wanted a fight and now it was going to get one.

19

Nothing seemed to make sense. Woody ran it all through the reels of his brain and nothing had made sense ever since they got to the fucking mine. Oh, he had fought against it with what he considered common sense and rationality, but even he had to face the ugly fact that something was terribly, terribly wrong here. Reality as he had known it his entire life had gone toes up.

He wandered through the darkened corridors of the building in search of Jerry, a guy he honestly really didn't like. That was the truth of the matter. He didn't like Jerry. He didn't really think anyone did. Funny him thinking that now. It had never truly occurred to him that he didn't like the guy. Jerry was someone he basically put up with.

But I hate him, he thought then. *I really, honestly hate the fucker. I hate that he has a girl like Marianna. That's what I hate most about him.*

Oh, that was stupid.

That was childish.

Why was he thinking something like that now? He moved down the corridor, guiding himself by his flashlight. If he hated him so much why was he risking his neck for him? But he knew. It was because he was a cop. And a cop didn't leave another cop behind...even one he couldn't stand. And nobody really liked Jerry. Even Dew had no real use for him. Maybe he had never said so, but Woody had sensed his displeasure with Jerry more than once. Jerry fucked up a lot. He made the wrong choices and came on heavy when he should have been light, acted like a tough guy when it was safe to do so and then lost his balls when the cards were down.

He was a useless fuck-up with a really good-looking girlfriend that he had no right to have in the first place—

Oh, fuck what is that?

It was on the wall. A dark smear. Glistening. Very red. Blood? Had to be. Somebody had come this way and left a smeared blood trail as if they had been bleeding very badly. Jerry?

It had to be Jerry. Woody shook his head. It didn't make sense. Hadn't he been down this corridor before? In fact, hadn't he been down it many times? His head was so mixed-up he just wasn't sure.

He wanted to run.

To get out of there because he really didn't trust what he was seeing. He didn't trust anything. He became aware of a smell, that same sweet intoxicating scent as before. It was a heady brew that he found nauseating.

Something brushed against his face and he cried out.

He had not imagined it. It felt like he had broken a cobweb with his face, a very large cobweb that was made of something much more resilient than silk. Fishing line maybe.

But there was nothing.

He followed the blood smear. It went on at irregular intervals as if whoever had left it kept bumping into the wall or maybe felt their way down it now and again with bloody hands.

"Jerry?" he said out loud. "Jerry?"

God, the sound of his voice. It echoed back at him through the emptiness, much louder, it seemed, than he had put it out.

The blood smear continued around the bend and then Woody saw where it stopped—at an open door. He could hear a gagging, moaning sound and he knew it was Jerry. There was something in its pitch. Sucking a breath into his lungs, he went through the doorway. What he saw in there nearly made him scream.

"Jerry?" he said.

There was a form crouched in the corner and judging by its size and the uniform it wore, it was most certainly his partner.

"Jerry?"

The figure lifted its head up and Woody saw that its face was smeared with blood. The redness was especially clotted and crusted around its mouth. *"Gaaaaaahhhhgaa,"* Jerry said, sobbing. *"Gaaaaaayaaa..."*

Woody put the light directly in his face and Jerry barely even blinked.

What the hell was wrong with him? That he was injured was obvious, but was his mind gone? Had he been stripped down to some infantile level where he was incapable of speech? No, that wasn't it. And as Jerry opened his mouth, Woody saw very clearly that he had no tongue.

Holy shit...somebody cut his fucking tongue out.

Now, he figured, was a good time to panic, but he wasn't giving into it. His horror and dismay and sheer revulsion at the situation made him want to scream, but that wasn't going to help anything. Especially poor Jerry. He reached down and took his hand and lifted him to his feet. He seemed very light as if he were stuffed with pillow down.

"Man, we'll get you help, but we have to get out of here, okay?"

Jerry nodded, his eyes huge and glassy.

"Stay with me," Woody told him. "Stay right behind me. We're leaving."

Gun in one hand and flashlight in the other, he led Jerry on down the corridor and around the bend, cutting forward and back until it seemed they would never get where they needed to go. But Woody knew what he was looking for and just ahead he found it: the office he had escaped from. They would go out the window and circle around to the parking lot. Fuck Dew. Fuck all this. This was no business for a handful of cops to take on, especially in the dead of night.

He slid his gun back in its holster, reaching out and taking Jerry by the hand...a hand that was still oily with blood and felt unpleasantly warm like meat that had been thawed in a microwave. Jerry made some horrible gobbling sounds that were the most heartbreaking and pathetic things that Woody had ever heard.

"It's okay, man. I'll get you out. I swear I will."

"Gah," Jerry managed. *"Gahhh-gah."*

Woody led him into the office. There was the open window and there was the way out. There really was nothing to it. Jerry pulled back as if he was afraid of what might be out there, but Woody calmed him with soothing tones the way he would a child and led him over there.

The only thing that stopped him from going through the window was a bumping sound. He turned quickly, shining his light in the direction of the noise…and gasped, drawing back. Across the room, there was a body hanging, its boots bumping against the wall as it swung back and forth. From the uniform it was wearing there was no doubt who it was.

Woody felt a raw and cutting panic open him up inside.

Jerry was pressed between him and the windowsill and he felt soft and spongy.

But it wasn't Jerry.

Because Jerry was hanging from the light fixture by his own tie, his neck broken, his face a web of blood.

And as Woody turned to face what was behind him, it grabbed him in flaccid hands and said, *"This is what it feels like when you fuck up, Woody."*

20

By the time Jay made it out of the crater, his heart seized in his chest and he thought he was going to die right there. Then it started again with a painful lurching and he stumbled forward, breathing hard, sweating, shaking.

It lured us down here, a voice in his head told him. *It manipulated us so easily.*

And it had, oh God yes, but it had.

As he started running, searching, looking for it, knowing he had to kill it, he could hear Tanya crying out in the distance. But he had no time for that. He had to find the thing and silence it before it told everyone about the secret, before Tanya figured out why his divorce had been so sudden and so ugly, before she blabbed to everyone about his stepdaughter and what he had done to her—

But how did it know? How could it know?

He kept running, moving in circles around heavy equipment and tool sheds and piles of gravel. It had lured him down here because it knew that he couldn't allow it to live, not with what it knew. The secret had to be kept secret. Yes, it had lured him here and when he went down in the crater and looked into the egg-shaped hollow, it had shown its true face to him and that's what made him scramble up the ladder. And worse, it had said things in his head, things he did not want anyone else knowing.

Behind him, footsteps.

He whirled around. There was nothing. Only clustering shadows that dissipated in the beam of the flashlight, slinking away like stark black rats. Gravel rolled down a hill. He turned again. Something brushed his back like ragged fingers. He turned around yet again, shaking, eyes bulging from his head.

"WHERE ARE YOU?" he demanded. "WHERE THE FUCK ARE YOU?"

There was a hot eruption of sweet gassy putrefaction that enveloped him and a voice that sounded much like the voice of Sofia, his stepdaughter, said, *"I'm right behind you, pervert."*

He whirled around and saw something like red claws streaking at his face and then a black shroud-like immensity fell over him.

21

As Tanya scrambled up the ladder to give chase to Jay, she made one colossal mistake. Even though a voice kept repeating in her mind that she should never, ever, under any circumstances look back, she did just that. Halfway up, the green fire licking from the hollow began to gain intensity, making the entire crater strobe and flicker, and she looked back to see what was happening.

She looked.

She saw.

Then she started screaming. Her entire body got into the act and with such overwhelming volition, that she lost her footing and dangled stupidly there by one hand, looking like a fly stuck to a No-Pest Strip. She saw what was coming out of the hollow and it nearly finished her. In her hysteria, she was certain that her brain would explode and fill her skull in a soup of blood. She was certain she would scream until her larynx ruptured. And she was certain that her mind was gone.

You're done, your race is run, you stupid fucking bitch! You let yourself be drawn down here and now here comes the thing that will suck your blood and eat your soul.

She tried to pull herself up the ladder, but her boots were muddy and she couldn't seem to get any traction. Same went for her hands. The filth caked on them acted like grease when she tried to get a good grip on the rungs.

And behind her, the thing grew larger. Like a balloon slowly being inflated, it filled itself with darkness and evil and her own shrieking subconscious terrors.

Not screaming now, but whimpering with abject horror, she scrambled frantically until she got the ladder under her, her boots gaining traction and propelling her up and up just as the fetid heat of the thing threatened to consume her.

As she dragged herself out of the crater on her belly, she could smell the sharp septic stench of the creature. It was feverish and rank like an open wound festering black with necrosis.

Then she was out, some deliriously happy voice in her head gibbering, *made it out, made it out, see I fucking well made it out.* She rolled over in the muck and splashed through a pink puddle and got to her knees. She still had her weapon and she drew it, knowing it wasn't going to do her much good but knowing she could not go down without a fight. It was important to fight back. If you went down on your knees at the sight of this thing, you'd never find your feet again.

So she brought up her weapon as the thing skittered up out of the crater.

In the yellow-orange sodium lights she saw it emerge and hover there at the edge indecisively. She wanted to scream again, but her throat was too raw. All that came out was a curious rasping, whistling noise. What she was looking at was not exactly the Spider from Mars she had seen earlier, but it was definitely an arachnid. It had to be, of course, because the fear of creepy-crawlies had been plucked from her mind by the thing and it wanted to devastate her with terror. So what better way?

It wasn't a spider, not really.

Maybe some abstract, expressionistic version of one, but no real spider was the size of a pickup truck nor could it ever have looked like this one. For one thing, it had four legs and spiders had eight. Its flesh was a mottled, indeterminate color—maybe brown going on gray, it was really hard to tell in the shadows— and jagged like plates of shattered glass welded into a serrated whole so that gleaming shards jutted from its legs and body in every which direction like knife blades. Beneath this, she saw glimpses of pale, wrinkled skin. There was a sort of segmented tail that it dragged behind it that bifurcated into a triple-pronged appendage from which wriggling things like glossy snakes dangled. Each of them licked the ground as if they were tasting it, much in the fashion of anteater's tongues. The front of the creature had two slender appendages hairy as vines that curled like question marks and set between them was a long knotted cord that projected out ten feet at least. At the end of which, there was a cup like the bulb of a flower and in it, a serous pink-yellow eyeball that stared out at her.

There was no mouth that she could see, but she did not doubt that it had one or that it wanted badly to introduce her to it.

Even as she leveled her weapon at it with one badly shaking hand, she could feel it trying to make contact with her, trying to worm its mind into her own. She likened it to a very wet, very slimy tongue sliding deep into her ear and licking her brain.

It was in.

There's only safety in me, it told her. She expected some grating horror movie voice but it was very melodic and almost sweet like that of a little boy. *Come to me, become part of me, lose yourself in what I am and never escape.*

But as sweet as the voice was, it was also exceedingly repellent and perverse.

"No!" she cried. *"No!"*

The spider-thing trembled at her defiance and it seemed to shrink back for a moment, then it let go with an agonized wailing in her head that seemed hypersonic. It made her brain reel. But it did not stop her from pulling the trigger which she did reflexively again and again. Slugs chewed into the beast and true to form, its plated armor cracked open and fell free like the glass of a broken mirror. She actually thought she was damaging it, hurting it, but it wasn't so.

It wasn't her bullets that made it fall apart.

It was molting.

Its jagged hide was cracking open with a sound much like ancient boards riddled with dry rot being yanked free of their nailheads, splintering and snapping. Its carapace finally split completely and Tanya saw legs coming out, the jointed legs of an insect but thorny like the stems of roses. There had to have been at least eight or nine of them. As it pulled its bulbous body free, she ran.

Sweating, whimpering, nearly struck mad by what she had just witnessed, she ran around piles of slag and cut between equipment sheds and crab-crawled up hills of gravel only to slide down into muddy pools on the other side. The thing was closing in on her and its stench was a horror unto itself. It contracted her throat, made her stomach convulse, and the breath wheeze in her lungs. She crept under the huge bulks of loaders and dump trucks, but felt too exposed. She had to hide. She had to find a hole.

But where?

Where?

She stumbled drunkenly, tripping and falling like some idiot in a horror movie. But the ground was uneven, rocky and cracked, set with hollows and clefts. There was the SUV. Thank God. She ran towards it and as she got there, she nearly broke down and started crying. It sat on four flat tires. There were other vehicles...but she knew nothing about driving big trucks and heavy equipment.

She was fucked.

She was done.

She was going to die.

And in the narrow, winding passages of her brain, she could hear the uppity I-told-you-so voice of Grandma Ruby. *Mmm-hmm. Now this is how it ends for you, child. Dirty, ugly, and horrible. That's what you get for mixing it up with whites. I saw it coming, but you wouldn't listen. Colored folks belong with colored folks and whites belongs with whites. Says so right in the Bible, but you wouldn't listen. Never would listen. Now it just ain't your body gonna get torn up but yer almighty soul. Shame on you, girl! Fer shame, fer shame!* Tanya clenched her teeth. She had no patience with that kind of thinking. Even in the grip of terror, it distressed her to no end.

"Fuck you," she said under her breath to Grandma Ruby's smug, wrinkled face.

She was not going to give in and she was not going to look behind her. She would find the road and get out of there on foot if she had to. Only she could hear the spider-thing behind her, tearing apart anything in its path. Sheds crashing down and trailers tipped over.

It was coming with a vengeance.

Ahead, she saw the line of bright blue shitters, the Port-O-Johns. There had to be a dozen of them. She could hide in one of them.

She ran over there...then skidded to a stop.

No, one of those would be like a coffin. She ran in the other direction and there was a great rumbling from beneath her that threw her to the earth. She broke her own rule, peering behind her. She saw one of the shitters vault up into the air and explode in a storm of plastic. Then a second one went and a third. One by one they erupted, a rain of filthy water, shit, piss, and chemicals raining down to earth along with the remains of the shitters themselves.

Tanya kept going, running, falling, dragging herself forward on her hands and knees. She saw a long white tool trailer. On its side in huge black letters was scrawled:

Nigger don't let the
Sun set on you here

She clambered to her feet, panting and crying. She could see the lights that marked the perimeter of the road. She had to get there. They wound up and up and up, winding along the sides of the pit until they reached the top. And as she saw this, with a sinking heart she saw them going out, one set after the other as if a series of switches were being thrown. Now the road leading out was completely black.

Then the lights went out in the pit.

She was in the utter blackness with the thing that was hunting her. She could hear it closing in, creeping forward on many legs. One single light was on, she saw. It marked the opening of a huge tunnel bored into the wall of the pit.

This is where she went.

Even though she knew she was making a terrible mistake.

22

When Dew got down to the bottom of the Empire Pit, he was in the darkness. The lights had gone out just as he turned onto the drive leading below which meant he had to take it slow and careful. And this while his guts felt like they were unraveling and his heart felt like it wanted to kick right out of his chest.

But he made it.

His nerves were frayed and he wouldn't have been surprised if his hair had gone from steel gray to pure white like in an old movie. He left the SUV running, the hi-beams on because they were the only light to be had. He grabbed his flashlight, a couple road flares, and the riot gun from its bracket, then stepped out into the darkest place on earth.

Right away, his handpack radio started crackling.

He ignored it because he knew there could be nothing good coming in on it. It had been dead all night. Even the SUV laptop was offline. The entity down here did not want its pets calling for help. It did not want that at all.

The radio crackled again and a voice which was clearly that of Jerry said, *"Dew, Jesus H. Christ, why did you let this happen? Why did you let that fucking thing do this to us? I know you never liked me...but you don't give a damn about Woody either? We were disposable? Cannon fodder? Goddamn lambs to the slaughter? Why, Dew? WHY? WHY THE FUCK WOULD YOU DO THIS TO US?"*

Dew nearly grabbed the radio and told Jerry how it wasn't true...but he knew it wasn't really Jerry. Maybe some impression the entity had culled from his mind or torn from his brain, but not Jerry. No way. As Dew explored the pit, his flashlight beam discovered the wreckage of the Port-O-Johns. The smell of shit and chemicals was thick in the air.

The entity kept raging over the handpack saying the most godawful things. Dew didn't bother shutting it off because he knew that he couldn't. When that thing wanted to blather on, nothing could shut it up. It kept trying to get his goat, turning the screw in his belly and working the knife in his back. It was trying to weaken him, tenderize him. Maybe some of what it said was true, but only some of it. True, he'd always preferred Woody because Woody was a better cop and he wasn't complaining all the time. He did his job well and could be extremely professional when the need arose. Jerry did his job, too, but he lacked any finesse. When you dealt with the public on a daily basis and not usually in their best form, you had to know how to tell people what they wanted to hear when they needed it most. Subtleties like that were lost on Jerry. Dew didn't even like to think of how many complaints he'd gotten from angry citizens about Jerry throwing f-bombs around and arguing with people, mouthing off to them and lecturing them. There was a lot more to being a good cop than pulling over speeders and dragging violent drunks from bars. A whole lot more.

"...and you always favored Woody, didn't you? He got the bread-and-butter and I got the fucking crust! He was like your little boy, your son, and the rest of us had to suck the root, take it and like it! Well, we DIDN'T like it! We hated you and your fucking favoritism—"

Dew knew that the entity was doing everything it could to prime him, to wring some negative emotion out of him, but it wasn't working. As it ranted on and on, he pulled the handpack radio from his belt and tossed it far into the distance. He heard it splash into a puddle.

There was satisfaction in that.

He kept going, distancing himself from the radio and the voice on it that still raged on and on. Now it was screaming, shouting, having an absolute tantrum.

"YOU LYING USELESS SCHEMING FUCK! DON'T YOU DARE TURN AWAY FROM ME! DON'T YOU DARE TRY TO SHUT ME OUT!" it shrieked, now in the voice of Dwight Rose. *"IT WAS YOUR FAULT! IT WAS ALL YOUR FAULT! I WAS RIGHT IN FRONT OF YOU! I WANTED YOU TO ARREST ME! I WAS BEGGING FOR YOU TO STOP ME WHEN THEY MADE ME DO IT!"*

Dew moved around several piles of rubble and the voice faded into the background. He was not entirely sure what his plan was or if he even had one. The only thing that seemed rock solid in his mind was that he had to do everything he could to frustrate the entity. He was more certain than ever it was a child of sorts and nothing pissed off a child more than being ignored.

You can't ignore me, he heard it say in his head. *You can't.*

He walked on, oblivious to the voice.

Did you hear me? Did you hear what I said to you?

Dew kept going, feeling himself growing strong. Because the stronger he was, the weaker the entity became. He had to remember that. Whatever else happened, it did not like strong people, willful people, people who were oblivious to its games. It did not like that at all.

DON'T YOU IGNORE ME! I'M HERE! I AM REAL! I AM ALL! YOU CANNOT REFUSE ME! YOU CANNOT SHUT ME OUT! I CAN KILL YOU ANYTIME I WANT!

"So kill me," Dew said out loud. "Go ahead. Because if you don't, I'm going to keep coming and coming and sooner or later I'll find you and I'll crush you under my boot."

Silence.

Deathly silence.

Then—

He saw a dark shape waiting for him. It was standing right in his path next to a fuel truck and whatever it was made of, it glistened like quartz. He felt a pang of fear like a blade cutting from his stomach up into his chest. *Don't falter. If you falter for one moment, you're finished.* So he did not falter. He walked straight at it until he was fifteen feet from it.

It came no closer.

He did not back down.

No, in fact, quite calmly, he bracketed his flashlight to the barrel of the riot gun and brought it up. He put the light right on the thing.

"Well, come on then," he said.

What faced him was an immense gray-green shape that looked much like a mammoth toad, one that was about the size of your average grizzly bear. It was warty and bumpy with bubble-like pustules that were a glossy white as if they were filled with pus. He could see it breathing. He could see the pustules breathing. He could see its immense golden eyes and register the whirpooling hate in them. It opened its mouth with a moist, slimy parting of slick membranes and made a guttural croaking sound. It had long glistening white teeth.

The teeth, oh dear God, those fucking teeth.

An image filled his mind. The toad had him. It had him by the head, pulling him deep into its mouth with a slavering, sucking sound. He was struggling, but it was no good. Its teeth were not letting him go. The toad's mouth parted wider and the jaws slid out like a drawer of knives, the teeth like fingers that walked down his spine as it gnawed on his head. Digestive juices gurgled from its flabby mouth and Dew felt his body shiver and go soft as rice pudding as the teeth walked down his back and the jaws pulled him deeper into the throat.

He shook it from his head.

He would not falter.

The toad hopped in his direction and he opened fire with the riot gun, blowing great shanks of toad-meat from it and permanently blinding one of its eyes. Bleeding an inky blood, it hopped away. He went after it and saw it disappear into a tunnel set in the pit wall.

It wants you to follow.

Dew knew it did.

Why the entity decided on a monster toad was beyond him. He knew he had to be careful because there was always the possibility it was toying with him, making him feel over-confident so it could use that against him.

Maybe.

Possibly.

Sucking in a deep breath, he followed the trail of toad slime into the tunnel, wondering if he'd ever get out again.

23

Tanya was crawling on her hands and knees through the tunnel which was not like some narrow mine crawlspace you saw on TV, but a huge passage that was strengthened by steel arches that reminded her of the rib bones of some prehistoric animal.

The lights in the tunnel which were strung in a long, seemingly unending line deep into the earth clicked on and off. Sometimes they did this in rapid succession like strobe lights, other times it was minutes in-between light and dark. Though in the back of her mind she realized that the point of this was to confuse her animal sense and disorientate her, all she could think of was the glaring pink light that exposed her and the silken darkness that sheltered her.

In the distance, she could hear a throbbing like a gigantic heart beating. And the farther she went in the tunnel, the closer she got to it. She didn't want that; the idea terrified her. But she could not retreat because the thing was behind her. Whatever it was would be horrible, she knew.

She paused.

She didn't know what to do.

She had been afraid for so long now, just devastated by mind-numbing terror, that she couldn't think straight. Nothing seemed to make sense and every decision seemed to be the wrong one. Sobbing under her breath, trembling, grimy and wet and feeling more like an animal than a human being, she pressed herself up against one of the arches where she shivered like a dog in the rain.

The lights went off.

"I'm so scared," she said in a low, pained voice. "I'm so scared."

She heard a clicking in her head and a voice said, *It's your own fault, child. You were always too headstrong and never would listen to good advice. Not a lick of common sense. Not a lick of it.*

She knew the voice was Grandma Ruby but Grandma Ruby was in a nursing home. She was in her nineties and pretty much out of touch with reality. Yet, this was certainly her voice.

The lights came back on.

Now you got yourself in a fix, don't you? No point in me telling you what to do. You know. You always got all the answers. I'll just shut my mouth because you like that best.

"No...no...please...I don't know...I don't know what to do," Tanya implored.

Well, you just can't sit there between heaven and hell. Hear the boom-boom-boom? That's where you need to get to. That's your sanctuary. You sit there much longer and that bad thing's gonna get you. Listen. You hear it? It's getting closer and it's gonna kill you.

The thing was, Tanya could hear it.

She could hear the steady *clomp-clomp-clomp* of its boots. And it was whistling. Yes, she was sure of it: it was whistling like a workman going about his job. She recognized it. The whistling was very melodic and the song was definitely "Working in the Coal Mine" which she had never really liked but now took on a much larger, darker dimension in her mind.

See? See? said Grandma Ruby. *It's coming for you and you better get! You hear? You better get!*

Out went the lights.

Filled with grief, anxiety, and an odd dreamlike terror, she got to her feet and started moving in the direction of the throbbing because that was sanctuary and God knew how much she needed sanctuary at that moment.

Hurry!

Yes, Tanya began moving faster with a stumbling gait. The tunnel canted downhill and it propelled her faster and faster and faster and she was going to make it. Then she stepped in a pothole, twisting her ankle, and she thought she heard Grandma Ruby cackling in her head—*tee-hee, tee-hee, teee-hee.* But Tanya wouldn't quit. Her ankle would not support her weight, but there were other ways. She dragged herself forward on her knees because she had to get to the bright spot ahead.

The lights came back on.

She felt a freezing shadow fall over her and she knew the game was up. She looked up and saw some grotesque thing standing there. It elicited a scream from her. There was no other reasonable reaction. It stood like a man, but its body was lumpy and swollen, its flesh spiraling and scalloped like the shell of a mollusk. It had a single huge eye that was like a ribbed vortex with a red pupil sitting in its center. And where its mouth should have been, there was a face. It was Jay's face, but rugose, veined like a leaf. It leaned over her until the Jay face was inches from her own.

"You listen to me now," it whispered as if it were sharing a secret from some dark, taboo midnight. *"What we have between us, Sofia, is private. It's personal. If you tell your mom, I'll have to hurt her. I'll have to hurt her real bad. And I'll make you watch. So keep your mouth quiet or things'll get real ugly. I'll do that thing to you that you don't like, the thing that hurts real bad...you get me? Are you reading me? That a big ten-four, Sofia? You understand me, you silly black wench, you dumb black twat?"*

Whimpering, hot tears rolling down her mud-crusted face, Tanya understood real well. She knew who Sofia was and she now knew why Jay's divorce had been so ugly that he refused to discuss it. He should have been in prison with the rest of the animals, but instead he was here, he was a monster and he was going to hurt her because there was no way she could keep her mouth shut.

As the Jay-thing reached down to take hold of her, she jabbed her finger into the soft pulp of the silver eye and a burning hot fluid splashed over the back of her hand.

The creature let go with a wild, resounding cry.

Oh, you treacherous bitch! Now I'll teach you, now I'll hurt you, now I'll fucking well school you! Oh, you're going to get yours! You're going to get a long, slow lickin' you won't forget.

But by then, Tanya was hobbling away, going deeper and deeper into the long dark tunnel and what waited at its end.

Nothing could stop her.

Nothing could be allowed to stand in her way.

She was standing up now. The agony in her ankle was incapacitating, yet she did not seem to feel it. She could only smell the sweet, syrupy secretions of what waited for her, of what needed her as much as she needed it. She hobbled along and the lights went off, then on, then off, going faster and faster until it was a flickering stroboscopic shadow show, but even this did not slow her down.

There was a place at the end of the tunnel, an opening and she found it, stumbling forward, her skin burning and her insides feeling like molten wax. Crying out gibberish, mindless and more aroused than she'd ever been in her life, she stripped her uniform off because she needed to feel the air buffeting her naked skin.

Hurry, Tanya, a voice called out to her. *Hurry or it'll be too late...you won't touch me and I won't touch you...*

The idea of that was like white-hot bolts of pain cutting through her. It dropped her to her hands and knees in the strobing light. She crawled, squirmed, and dragged herself forward until she fell into a hollow and a squeaking voice in her brain sang, *Tanya Seatin, Tanya Seatin, won't be happy until she's eaten!* And then she was psychically seized and brought into the fold of something immense and oily. Her eyes rolled back white in her head and her mouth was filled with a peculiar dark, sour sweetness which was the taste of fear and sex, death and pain and passion. She could barely breathe. She was overwhelmed by surging adrenaline and rioting beta-endorphins and the heady onrush of hormones. Gasping and crying out, she reached out to touch the throbbing thing which had called her down the birth canal of the tunnel into this steaming, sucking pit of organic profusion. She felt a greasy, rubbery flesh that was taut as the belly of a pregnant woman in her eighth month. It pulsated under her fingertips, exuding a yolky sap that made her hands burn with needle-prick eruptions of tactile delight. Her fingertips found something else, an orifice that was soft like juicy fruit pulp that she not only wanted to touch, but *needed* to touch.

Chemical fireworks exploded in her like stars being born and black nebulas being sucked into themselves, worm-holing through her subconscious and making the neurons of her hypothalamus light up with frantic electrical activity. Her teeth chattered and her mouth drooled. Her limbs jerked, her body convulsed, and her labia burned like a match head as she rode an arcing current of primal sexual energy. She pressed herself up against the thing, each throbbing beat of it releasing orgasms in her that sapped her willpower and turned her thoughts to mush.

Something gasping and giggling in her, she pressed her spasming body against the thing, gripping it with clawing fingers and ramming her hips against its bulk, crying out as its tiny needling spines pierced her, injecting her with pheromones that erased any idea in her brain that she was an individual.

Now she was part of it; she belonged to it.

She pressed her mouth to its flesh, its warm greasy secretions making her lips pull back against clenched white teeth. She licked it and it tasted like the sweetest golden spongecake. Her tongue explored the creature's flesh, licking into minute folds and pockets of tissue, tasting white sugar and black blood, salty meat and smooth bone.

The creature moved against her.

It quivered.

It quaked.

Then it responded in kind, something like serpents licking along her legs and exploring the cleft at her ass. They roiled and boiled over her, a baptismal of greedy tongues. One of them slid through her cupped hand and it felt the way she imagined a skinned snake might feel, soft and moist and undulant.

Tanya Seatin, Tanya Seatin, won't be happy until she's eaten! This I say and keep repeatin'! the voice chanted in the emptiness of her brain, rhythmic and captivating.

Drool dripping from her mouth, sweat erupting from her pores like lava, she clutched the forest of tongues, felt them lick like suckering mouths over her breasts and belly and thighs. Then one of them entered her and another corkscrewed up her ass and she writhed with agony as the devouring began. More of them rammed up inside her, fighting for space as others filled her mouth and slid up her nostrils and popped her eyes from their sockets as they sought to plant themselves in the hothouse soil of Tanya Seatin.

She would have screamed had she not been filled, but maybe it wouldn't have been heard over the cracking of her bones from internal pressure or the sheering of her skin or the pistol-shot splintering of her spine that twisted into a helix until it shattered. In the end, she was glued to the creature, melted to it, a river that washed over it.

Tanya no longer existed, save as a delicate brown bud that grew from the seedy underbelly of her tormentor. And the hunger that still lived in the wreckage of her body wouldn't have wanted it any other way.

24

The tunnel slowly angled down and from the looks of it—when the lights were on—it was not an old channel but something comparatively recent. It was very large, spacious and airy. It ran for about a hundred feet and then terminated at an arched opening at the end.

But what was it for?

What was its purpose?

Somebody must have dug it out for some reason.

These things echoed through Dew's brain as he walked through intermittent light and darkness. He felt a terrible magnetism to what was waiting for him down there. True, the tunnel moved downwards at a slight incline so gravity was pushing him faster towards the end, but there was more to it than that. Much more. He found that he was walking faster and faster and then even faster. His mouth was dry. His heart was hammering. His palms were sweating. As much as he knew there was nothing but horror waiting for him, he had never wanted to get anywhere so badly in his life.

Now he was jogging.

And as he jogged, he realized that he was grinning. The smile was etched deep in his face and there was a low, near-hysterical laughter coming up the back of his throat.

This is it, this is it, this is it, a voice in his head informed him. *This is what you've been waiting for your entire life. This is the big one. This is the payoff and the climax, the atomic bomb of orgasms.*

And as he rushed forward and ever downwards, to meet his destiny, he knew it was true just as he knew his mind was beginning to splinter in his head from the hypnotic, addictive pull of the thing that waited for him. He could smell the sweet, sweet, sugary promise that made him giddy, made him feel like he could walk on air and tap-dance on the ceiling of the tunnel.

Oh God, I'm almost there, I'm almost there—

Then the archway opened and some intellectual part of his brain that saw through the mists and analyzed what was fed to it by his senses informed him that there was symbolism here. That this in its own horrendously twisted way was like a repetition of the birth experience and he was pushing, pushing so damn hard to get through that arch because he wanted the light at the end of the tunnel, he wanted revelation, he needed to see and feel what it was all about.

Then he was through.

There was a huge circular chamber before him and the lights didn't go out at all because what was in here wanted him to see.

In the center of the chamber, about sixty feet from the archway, there was a bowl-like depression and a flickering blue-green glow coming from it. Yes, this was the epicenter, this was the heart and he could hear it throbbing in his head.

He started walking towards it and there were things around him that looked oddly like transparent dry cleaning bags, though bunched and wrinkled. There were six or seven of them. He could see a dark, hunched-over shape in each. He prodded one of them with the barrel of the riot gun and it gave quite easily. It was soft and rubbery almost like a water balloon sloshing and half-full.

He stood there, swallowing down something inside him.

A chrysalis, he thought. *The chrysalis of a moth or a butterfly.*

The sweet, intoxicating odor and the need to look into the bowl-like depression had waned now for here was a mystery and his innate cop's curiosity did not like mysteries. He had to know what was in those sacks.

He had to.

Down on his knees, he set aside the riot gun and pulled a lock-blade knife from his pocket. He jabbed one of the bags and its texture was very tough, very resilient, but he was determined. He kept stabbing it until he pierced it. It split open and a watery discharge that stank hot and acrid gushed out. Along with a human hand. There was a body in the bag. He pulled it free and saw that it was a young guy, twenty-something. He convulsed in

Dew's arms, eyes flickering, then he vomited out a quantity of the fluid.

And died.

Dew opened another bag. An older man, white-haired, wearing a suit and tie. He likewise convulsed and puked out that fluid and died.

Dew stepped away, wet with the stuff, shaking and trying to comprehend what he was seeing. But the answer was obvious. These were the miners and Superior's managers. The entity had put them in these bags. And judging by the quantity of deflated bags over near the depression, the entity was using them like Ziploc storage bags—it was keeping its snacks in them. Keeping them fresh. It was getting ready to divide and like an infant, it needed to feed almost continually until it was strong enough for the process.

Dew, feeling numb now and beyond simple animal fear, moved amongst the bags until he reached the lip of the depression. He looked down into the hollow. He was expecting some ultra-fast, ultra-wiry, spider-like creature, but that's not what he saw at all. The entity was huge and bloated. It must have weighed several tons, a flaccid, pulsating monstrosity that looked very much like some gargantuan, engorged, overfed tick. It throbbed like a dying heart in its nest of shrunken, leeched human corpses. It was so fat that its spiny jointed legs looked vestigial. They were curled beneath it, incapable of animating the fleshy mass of corruption they were anchored to.

It had eyes.

Huge eyes like glossy soap bubbles and with these it stared up at Dew with anger, with wrath, with utter hate. It shivered as it tried to lift itself up, its body quivering like a soft-boiled egg, distended and blubbery and oozing a gray sap. It pulled itself up and Dew saw there were pulsing sacks attached to it...save they weren't sacks but *people*.

There were fifteen or twenty of them.

They hung off the creature like swollen polyps, living human bags that expanded and deflated as if breathing, stretching to the point that it looked as if they might explode then shrinking into wrinkled envelopes like garments drooping on hangars. And the most obscene thing about it all was that their mouths were grinning, pink tongues licking sallow lips, faces etched with looks of pure orgasmic delight that only increased when they inflated.

This is what Dew saw.

This is what tapped the strength from him when he needed it most.

Come down to me, Dew, its voice moaned in his head. *You must come down and be part of me.*

The creature, the entity, rose up from the hollow as if it were going to attack, but it was noticeably sluggish, top-heavy and enormously swollen. As it fought to rise up, Dew saw that its underbelly was set with dozens of wriggling hoses that were like the trunks of elephants, sagging and wrinkly, and at the end of each was a set of full red lips and a suckering mouth of tiny teeth like fish bones. The hoses moved like fingers, flexing and lengthening. Between their multiple rows was a vast mouth-like crevice that opened to reveal inward-curving, hooked teeth. Slime ran in gouts from it. Inside the mouth itself, it looked hairy and stringy like the guts of a pumpkin.

It lurched forward.

Dew went down on his ass because he knew he was a dead man...then the creature sank back into the pit. He didn't know what it was all about. Not right then. Slowly, he climbed to his feet and the chamber rumbled from the weight of the entity, nearly sending him headlong into its lair.

Why wasn't it attacking?

Why wasn't it killing him?

Why wasn't it attacking his mind at the very least?

As he watched it, bringing up the riot gun, it settled into the cavity its bulk had created. Right away, it began to foam with some gurgling secretion. It covered itself in a thick membrane of translucent jelly.

In his mind, he heard his own voice saying: *It's one cell but if you don't get a handle on it, it's going to start dividing and there'll be two and then four and then eight and then sixteen and thirty-two and sixty-four—*

Yes, it was splitting.

That's why it wasn't attacking—it didn't have the strength. The terror cell was in the process of division. It was torpid, weak, sated, and lazy with the energy it was using to split itself. It didn't have the strength to so much as swat at him. Beneath the fluctuating translucent membrane, he could see it happening. Its mass was shifting, pulling away from itself. It was shadowy, but apparent. Except...

Except it wasn't splitting into two hemispheres, but into three. This wasn't binary division, it was trinary: it was splitting into *three* entities.

And when it was complete, it would rise up, a trinity of horror and unbelievable menace. One of them had taken the mine and dozens of its workers. Three of them would take the nearest town which was Mineral City. Then, the three of them, stuffed full of human meat and blood, gluttonous and lazy from stuffing themselves on human suffering, would divide again and there would be nine of them and then twenty-seven and—

Dew started firing with his riot gun, but the gluey slime that enveloped the creature was impervious to buckshot. He lit one of the road flares and tossed it down there. It sizzled and went out like a cigarette in a mud puddle. The membrane was a protective covering. It could not be breached.

At least by ordinary means.

If you're going to do something, he thought then, *you better do it right goddamn now. When it finishes, you don't stand a chance.*

He ran out of the chamber and into the tunnel.

He kept running until he was out in the rain again, out in the pit. The fuel truck was there. It was waiting. A big old Seneca. He had driven one before he was a cop. Its tank would hold at least 4000 gallons. The fact that it was still down in the pit made him think that it had not been emptied yet, that it was still full of diesel fuel. He was counting on it. He opened the door. The keys were in the ignition. It was a spot of luck, but, then again, why wouldn't they be? Who would sneak into the mine and all the way down to the bottom of the pit to steal a fuel truck?

He turned it over.

It coughed, but caught.

Now was the time. He put it in gear and began his roll to the tunnel.

25

As he drove down the tunnel towards the archway, Dew wondered if the chamber down there had been gouged out to be used as a fuel depot. It seemed likely. He drove on and on, his anxiety ramping up along with his nerves and he wondered if he'd have the guts to do what needed doing. The possibility of living through it was slim.

You worry about that later, if there is a later. Right now you do the right thing.

In his mind, that made perfect sense.

He pulled the truck through the arches, thinking about Woody and Jerry and how the night had started out so damn ordinary. Which only went to prove, he figured, that the world you woke up to in the morning was not necessarily going to be the same one you saw at the end of the day. People woke up every day feeling chipper only to be laid low by a stroke or heart attack by noon or to die in a car accident or from an embolism by suppertime. It happened every day. You kissed your husband good-bye when he went to work and by evening you were a widow. You got your children on the bus at first light and by day's end you were childless. Fate was reaching out to destroy you every minute and take away everything you ever cared about or lived for.

So if you could choose your own end, there was something satisfying in raising a middle finger to fate, destiny, or God above.

A split second after he drove through the arches, Dew stomped down on the accelerator. He plowed through the bodies in the bags, smashing them aside like sacks of trash. When he was within twenty feet of the hollow, every muscle in his body standing taut, he felt rather than heard the creature's mind wake up, struggling out of dormancy because it knew what he was doing.

YOU DON'T DARE! it cried out in rage inside his mind. *YOU DON'T DO THIS TO ME! TO US! TO THE ALL!*

But he *was* doing it and the creature roared/screamed/screeched with rising fury and absolute wrath. But even so, it was weak, it was still dreaming, it didn't have the tools to fight with. Inside the protective encapsulation of its membrane, it was literally caught with its pants down and there really wasn't a damn thing it could do except—

The truck vaulted into the hollow, tearing right into the thing and bursting its membrane and doing irreparable damage to the process of division. The three were not complete yet and the terror cell screeched in agony as the truck ripped into it, smashing down on its swollen mass with tons of iron.

The impact would have tossed Dew right through the windshield had he not been belted in. As it was, the cab was filled with sheets of glass. The driver's side door exploded off its hinges as the truck flipped over and then rolled on its side.

Dew went out cold.

When he came to, it was to the gagging stench of diesel fuel. His idea had been to drive the truck in there and then open the discharge valve, emptying the tank into the hollow. But apparently that wasn't necessary.

Gagging on the fumes, he couldn't seem to get his belt loose. Fuck it.

He pulled out his lock-blade knife and sawed through the straps until he was free. He fell out the missing door, landing in a pool of diesel fuel that was rapidly rising. Shrunken corpses floated in it. He scrambled towards the wall of the hollow, his head spinning. Behind him, he heard the entity thrashing against the truck, finally flipping it over and freeing itself. It was damaged, gutted, but it was far from finished.

Dew climbed up out of the hollow as he heard the creature dragging itself after him.

He made it fifteen feet away, lit his last road flare and tossed it into the hollow. At the same moment he flung it, he ran full out towards the archway. He was almost there, dreading that the flare had missed its target, when there was an incredible eruption of force and heat and the shock wave tossed him through the archway and right into the earthen wall on the other side, knocking the wind out of him.

He crawled on his hands and knees, scrambling down the tunnel as a cloud of fire belched from the archway, burning away half of the hair on his head.

He found his feet and started running, smoldering and blackened, choking on smoke and fumes, stumbling forward in the darkness. The explosion had turned off the lights, but the tunnel was lit by the orange glow of the blazing chamber.

He heard the waning, weakened cry of the entity as the fire consumed it, turning its birth chamber into a crematory. Its voice echoed into nothingness, fading with an almost human note of terror and pain.

Dew knew he was nearing the end of the tunnel.

It wouldn't be long.

He was almost there.

Then a tremor threw him off his feet. The tunnel shook and the earth heaved and he knew he wasn't getting out of there. There was a resounding explosion behind him—maybe the fuel truck itself going up, maybe a pocket of subterranean gas had ignited—and then the iron arches holding up millions of tons of rock and earth buckled and collapsed. In the split second before he was flattened by a shelf of bedrock the size of a three-story house, Dew heard the sneering, cynical voice of the entity in his mind say, *This is my place and my time and nobody gets out alive.* And it was true, it was really true, but Dew smiled, thinking, *Not even you, you sonofabitch, because I got you.* Then the wall of the pit moved like a mountain and he knew no more.

—The End—

CHECK OUT OTHER GREAT HORROR NOVELS

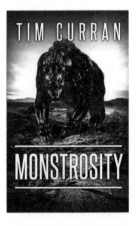

MONSTROSITY
by Tim Curran

The Food. It seeped from the ground, a living, gushing, teratogenic nightmare. It contaminated anything that ate it, causing nature to run wild with horrible mutations, creating massive monstrosities that roam the land destroying towns and cities, feeding on livestock and human beings and one another. Now Frank Bowman, an ordinary farmer with no military skills, must get his children to safety. And that will mean a trip through the contaminated zone of monsters, madmen, and The Food itself. Only a fool would attempt it. Or a man with a mission.

THE SQUIRMING
by Jack Hamlyn

You are their hosts

You are their food.

The parasites came out of nowhere, squirming horrors that enslaved the human race. They turned the population into mindless pack animals, psychotic cannibalistic hordes whose only purpose was to feed them.

Now with the human race teetering at the edge of extinction, extermination teams are fighting back, killing off the parasites and their voracious hosts. Taking them out one by one in violent, bloody encounters.

The future of mankind is at stake.

And time is running out.

CHECK OUT OTHER GREAT HORROR NOVELS

BLACK FRIDAY
by Michael Hodges

Jared the kleptomaniac, Chike the unemployed IT guy, Patricia the shopaholic, and Jeff the meth dealer are trapped inside a Chicago supermall on Black Friday. Bridgefield Mall empties during a fire alarm, and most of the shoppers drive off into a strange mist surrounding the mall parking lot. They never return. Chike and his group try calling friends and family, but their smart phones won't work, not even Twitter. As the mist creeps closer, the mall lights flicker and surge. Bulbs shatter and spray glass into the air. Unsettling noises are heard from within the mist, as the meth dealer becomes unhinged and hunts the group within the mall. Cornered by the mist, and hunted from within, Chike and the survivors must fight for their lives while solving the mystery of what happened to Bridgefield Mall. Sometimes, a good sale just isn't worth it.

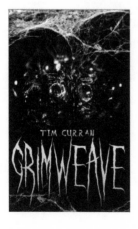

GRIMWEAVE
by Tim Curran

In the deepest, darkest jungles of Indochina, an ancient evil is waiting in a forgotten, primeval valley. It is patient, monstrous, and bloodthirsty. Perfectly adapted to its hot, steaming environment, it strikes silent and stealthy, it chosen prey: human. Now Michael Spiers, a Marine sniper, the only survivor of a previous encounter with the beast, is going after it again. Against his better judgement, he is made part of a Marine Force Recon team that will hunt it down and destroy it.

The hunters are about to become the hunted.

CHECK OUT OTHER GREAT HORROR NOVELS

DEATH CRAWLERS
by Gerry Griffiths

Worldwide, there are thought to be 8,000 species of centipede, of which, only 3,000 have been scientifically recorded. The venom of Scolopendra gigantea—the largest of the arthropod genus found in the Amazon rainforest—is so potent that it is fatal to small animals and toxic to humans. But when a cargo plane departs the Amazon region and crashes inside a national park in the United States, much larger and deadlier creatures escape the wreckage to roam wild, reproducing at an astounding rate. Entomologist, Frank Travis solicits small town sheriff Wanda Rafferty's help and together they investigate the crash site. But as a rash of gruesome deaths befalls the townsfolk of Prospect, Frank and Wanda will soon discover how vicious and cunning these new breed of predators can be. Meanwhile, Jake and Nora Carver, and another backpacking couple, are venturing up into the mountainous terrain of the park. If only they knew their fun-filled weekend is about to become a living nightmare.

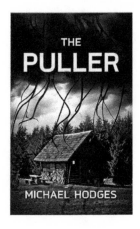

THE PULLER
by Michael Hodges

Matt Kearns has two choices: fight or hide. The creature in the orchard took the rest. Three days ago, he arrived at his favorite place in the world, a remote shack in Michigan's Upper Peninsula. The plan was to mourn his father's death and figure out his life. Now he's fighting for it. An invisible creature has him trapped. Every time Matt tries to flee, he's dragged backwards by an unseen force. Alone and with no hope of rescue, Matt must escape the Puller's reach. But how do you free yourself from something you cannot see?

CPSIA information can be obtained
at www.ICGtesting.com
Printed in the USA
LVHW032342220119
604913LV00002B/254/P